DL GALLIE

Edited by **Karen Hrdlicka**, Barren Acres Editing

Cover by **Ally Hastings,** Star Crossed Designs

Proofread by **Heart Full of Reads Editing Services**

Interior formatting by **DL Gallie**

Synopsis

There's a fine line between love and hate.
And a love fuelled from hate, is the strongest of them all.

BAYLOR
My life hasn't gone as I planned, but it's all my doing.
I'm given a second chance.
But I didn't count on him—Agent Corey Cox.
He's on the straight and narrow, abiding by the rules.
He calms my inner beast and makes me want to be a better person.
When my past reappears, that wildness inside sparks to life again.
Is his love enough to stop me turning my back on everything I've worked so hard for?

COREY
I live my life by the book.
Being an agent is everything to me.
The lines are never blurred.
Until her—Baylor Evans.
She's wild, carefree, and marches to the beat of her own drum.
She brings out a side to me I never knew existed.
When the past catches up with us, everything implodes.
Is my love for her enough? Or will I lose it all?

Playlist

Anywhere - Rita Ora
Purple Rain - Prince
Unstoppable - Sia
The Last Time - The Script
Bitch - Meredith Brooks
Born this Way - Lady Gaga
You're The one I Want - Loving Calibre
Sober - Demi Lovato
Stronger - Kelly Clarkson
Love the Way You Lie - Eminem feat. Rhianna
When Love and Hate Collide - Def Leppard
What About Now - Daughtry
ICH TU DIR WEH - Rammstein
Set Fire to the Rain - Adele
I Knew Your Were Trouble - Taylor Swift
Butterfly - Crazytown
Story of my Life - One Direction
True Colours - Cyndi Lauper
Apologise - Timberland
Dusk Till Dawn - ZAYNE feat. Sia

Not in Love - Olin and the Moon
The Reason - Hoobastank
Animals - Maroon 5
Girl on Fire - Alicia Keys
Sweet but Psycho - Ava Max
The Diary of Jane - Breaking Benjamin
Broken - Seether feat. Amy Lee
I'll Stand by You - The Pretenders
FourFiveSeconds - Astrid S
Maneaster - Hall & Oats
Nothing Like Them - Loving Calibre
Better Than Me - Hinder
Without You - Hinder
You and Me - Lifehouse
Bring me to Life - Evanesence
Hey Hey, My My - Battleme
Way Down We Go - KALEO
Bad Reputation - Joan Jett and the Blackhearts
Cruel to be Kind - Letters to Cleo
Can't Take my Eyes off You - Frankie Valli
Even Angels Fall - Jessica Riddle
The Weakness in Me - Joan Armstrong
My Happiness - Powderfinger
Iria - The Goo Goo Dolls

This playlist can be found Spotify.

"The course of true love never did run smooth"

~ *William Shakespeare*

Prologue

"TIME'S UP, BITCH," he snarls at me, "Time to choose who lives...and who dies." While delivering the ultimatum, his tone changes to sinister and downright frightening, especially on those last four words; how I was ever in love with this man—no, monster— is beyond me.

"No," I cry, my eyes flicking between them. The choice before me is impossible. The old me would've easily chosen in a heartbeat, consequences be damned, but the new me? Well, she cares. She has a heart now. She worries about things and people.

No matter what I choose right now, someone will die. Someone I care for will lose their life and there's nothing I can do to stop it.

My gaze darts between the two people who mean the most to me in this world. *How do I choose?* And then it hits me; I know what to do. "Me," I whisper.

"What?" he growls, spittle flying from his lips.

"Me," I quietly whisper. "I choose me," I say, louder this time, my voice clear and firm. The ramifications of my decision yet to sink in.

"No!" they both cry out.

"It's the only way," I reaffirm.

Looking back to *him*, I stare into his evil eyes. "I. Choose. Me," I confidently say, enunciating each word to prove my point. There's not a hint of hesitation in my voice; in reality, it's the complete opposite of how I really feel, but it's the only way to protect them. It's a sacrifice I'm willing to make. My death means they will live.

"Very well then." He raises his pistol and points it directly at me. My heart races as I stare down the barrel of his gun.

With death literally staring me in the eyes, a calmness washes over me as I wait. Closing my eyes, I breathe in deeply for the last time.

I'm ready.

His snicker pierces the silence and that sound grates through me. He clicks the safety and then all hell breaks loose.

Gunfire rings all around me. The sound is deafening as bullets fly around, and then it's silent.

Dead silent.

I'm frozen on the spot, waiting for death to take me. Waiting for the pain of being shot to register, but it doesn't come. Everything around me is moving in slow motion. Everything around me is fuzzy. I'm blinking rapidly to clear my vison but it doesn't clear. My heart rapidly races at the unknown.

In the distance, I vaguely hear voices and shouting but it's all muffled. In the blink of an eye, everything comes roaring back to life in high definition and surround sound.

I can hear the people around me shouting and running. The birds chirping in the trees nearby. The water lapping at the shore end, and then it hits me; I'm still standing.

I'm still alive.

Looking down, that's when I see it. My eyes widen at the scene before me. Tears begin to flow down my cheeks. My vision blurs as more liquid leaks from my eyes. I collapse to my knees and fall to the deck. I stare into lifeless eyes.

Someone is shouting my name but darkness is encroaching and engulfing me. It's pulling me under and I'm powerless to stop it.

My last thought before I drift into the dark abyss is they are dead…and it's all my fault.

CHAPTER 1

Corey

STANDING IN THE ADJOINING ROOM, I stare through the two-way glass, flicking the mic switch on. I smirk when I hear her going off at the agent. With his back to me, I'm not sure who it is. I turn it off and shake my head; Baylor Evans has a smart and sassy mouth. From watching her just now, she intrigues me and I'm not sure if that's a good thing or not, especially with what I'm about to propose to her.

She's sitting at the table across from the agent, her clothes are torn, her hair is a mess, and her face is bruised and swollen. From what I can gather, she's been through a lot in the last four days. My eyes are locked on her. This woman has been at the forefront of my mind, ever since the boss handed me the file with her picture in it. I've stared at the photo more than I should have, and I've memorized every inch of her face and body: blonde hair, blue eyes, super fit, a killer rack—hey, I'm a boob man, shoot me. In three words, she's fucking hot, and just the person I need to wrap this case up.

Picking up the file, I go over it one more time, not that I need to because I know it word-for-word and back-to-front. I've been on the Vlahos case for eighteen months now, and this is the first positive lead I've had fall into my lap.

Looking back up, I watch her. She's angry right now, I need her to calm down before I approach her and offer her the deal of her life.

The door opens and in walks Agent Oats. "Oats," I say in greeting, shaking his hand.

"Cox," he replies, and knocks on the glass garnering the attention of his partner, Agent Hall. Yes, their names are Agent Hall & Oates—great, now I'm fucking humming "Maneater" by the famous duo.

Hall stands up and exits the interrogation room to join us. When he opens the door, we hear her. "You fucking dick-wads, you can't keep me locked up. I was just kidnapped for fuck's sake. I have fucking rights. You ass—"

He pulls the door shut. "Fuck me," he mumbles, as he leans against the door he just closed.

"Well, she seems fun," I say, as I offer him my hand. He takes my outstretched hand and shakes it. "She's kind of a wild kitten with no filter, hey?"

"More like a foul-mouthed, fucking out of control tiger." The three of us laugh.

"You sure about this plan, Cox?" Oats asks me.

Nodding my head, I turn around and lean against the glass, crossing my legs at the ankle, while resting my palms on the window ledge. "Yep, Baylor Evans has the in that I need."

"But she's a live wire," Hall retorts.

"Exactly, she's perfect," silently I add, *in every-fucking-way,* "and that's why they won't suspect a thing."

"It's your career," he throws back at me. "But first, you need to convince psycho Barbie in there to cooperate with your crazy plan."

Turning around, I stare at her before turning my attention back to him. "Are you doubting my ability, Hall?"

"Fuck yes, I am. That woman is a time bomb waiting to explode, Cox. I hope you know what you're doing." With that, he and Oats walk out, leaving me alone.

Taking a deep breath, I pick up the file, a box, and open the door. I step into the danger zone, also known as the interrogation room.

"About fucking…" she snarls and stops when she sees it's me and not Hall. "Who the fuck are you?"

"Watch your mouth," I warn.

"Fuck you," she spits back at me.

I raise my eyebrows at her and she flips me the bird. Shaking my head, I walk farther into the room. "I'm Agent Corey Cox."

"Where's dumbass?"

"Not here," I say, taking a seat across from her. I slide the box over to her.

"What the fuck is this?"

"What have I said about your language, Ms. Evans?"

She rolls her eyes at me and we silently stare at each other across the table, assessing one another. The longer we stare, the thicker the air becomes in the room. *She really is more stunning in person. Focus, Cox, focus.*

"Well?" she sasses.

"Open it and see."

She eyes me suspiciously. I stare back at her, not giving anything away.

Finally she gives in and lifts the lid, her eyes widen in surprise. "How do you know that Grape Laffy Taffy is my favorite?" she asks, as she grabs a piece of candy and begins to unwrap it.

"It's my job to know everything about those I'll be working with."

She has the piece halfway to her lips, and asks, "What the fuck are you talking about?" She pops the taffy into her mouth and begins to chew…loudly…like a fucking horse.

"As I said before, Ms. Evans, watch the language, please."

"Oh, are you the swearing police now, Agent-whatever-you-said-your-name-was?" She pauses, her eyes roam over me, trying to determine why I'm here. My thoughts are confirmed when she asks me, "What's this all about?"

"You and I are going to be working closely to bring down Kye Vlahos and his organization."

Her face drops at the mention of Kye, and it confirms to me she really has no idea he's still alive.

"Kye's dead," she whispers flatly.

"You sure about that?" Opening the file, I grab a surveillance photo taken three days ago and slide it across the metal table to her.

She picks it up and when she looks at it, her eyes bug wide open. "How? What? Why? This is a trick. You're fucking with me."

"No trick, Ms. Evans. And I'm not fucking with you either. Seems lover boy left you out of the loop and kept something pretty significant from you. Kye Vlahos is very much alive and well. His doppelgänger however, well, he's dead."

"What?" she says, her tone shocked at the doppelgänger revelation.

"Do you know who Kye Vlahos really is?"

"Obviously, I don't because I thought he was dead, but from that photo, clearly," she sasses, "he's not."

"Mr. Vlahos is THE king of the drug trade on the East Coast and head of the Vlahos dynasty. He faked his death to throw us, and his family off his trail, but we have eyes and ears everywhere, and well, you can guess the rest. We knew he was still alive, we just didn't know why or how or where he was hiding out. That was until he got cocky. He reappeared in person a few days ago. He's looking for someone." I pause for effect. "That someone...is you!" Her mouth drops open at this revelation, "He's been following you for weeks now, Ms. Evans. Well, his lackey, Creed

Dawson, has been following you. Seems like Kye misses you."

"He's dead," she whispers, shaking her head. "I saw them kill him. I saw it with my own fucking eyes," she says, still staring at the photos of her not-so-dead ex-lover. She lifts her head to look at me. "Are you fucking with me?"

"Mouth. As I've already said, I'm not messing with you. You saw what they wanted you to see. And he wanted you, us, and everyone else to think he was dead."

She throws the photo on the table and starts shaking her head from side to side. "That fucking, dickwad, psycho asshole," she snaps, standing up, and slamming her palms on the table in anger. "I'm going to kill that fucker myself when I find him—"

"That's not the plan I have in mind," I tell her.

"Fuck you and fuck your plan. No one tells me what to do."

"Watch your mouth."

"Go fuck yourself, Cox."

"Do you want your sister to get hurt again?" I know it's a low blow using her sister like that, but I need Baylor if I'm going to crack this case.

Her heads snaps up toward me and if I thought she was angry before, she's furious now. "Leave my sister out of this," she growls between clenched teeth. "She has nothing to do with this."

"She became a part of this as soon as you did. You do realize she ended up in hospital because of *you*? They thought she was you. You don't want that to happen again, do you? Kye clearly wants you back and you are going to willingly go back to him because you are going to help me bring him and his organization down."

"And why would I do that?"

"Because it will shave time off your sentence and it will bring down the biggest drug racket since Pablo Escobar in the nineties."

"Why me?"

"Because you're our—well my—only hope." I tell her honestly.

She sits back down and picks up the surveillance photo. She stares at it and then quietly asks, "Can you promise me my sister will be safe?" She lifts her gaze to mine. Her face is etched with worry, but I think it's for her sister and not for herself. This woman is hard to read, which is why she's perfect for this undercover assignment. "I won't do this if she's at risk. I can't and won't let her get hurt again."

"I will do everything in my power to protect her but I can only do that if you agree to help me."

She stares at me and I have no fucking clue if she's going to help me or not. She grabs another candy and slowly opens it. She pops it into her mouth and chews. The silence, well apart from her chewing, is deafening.

Finally, she breaks the silence, shocking me when she agrees. "I'll do it, but if even a hair on my sister's head is touched or out of place, I will fucking chop your balls off and feed them to you, drenched in hot sauce."

"My, my, you're a feisty little kitten."

"Fuck you, Buster," she snarls, the tone of her voice and her sass turning me on, but at the same time, I'm convinced that given the chance, she absolutely would chop my balls off in a heartbeat.

"Meow," I sass before turning around and walking out of the room. Slamming the door behind me, I lean against the wood and let out a deep breath. A grin appears on my face and I shake my head, this case sure just got interesting.

CHAPTER 2

Baylor

STARING at the door Agent Cox just walked out of, I shake my head in disbelief. My mind is racing. The last week has been crazy, like something from a movie. First, I pretended to be my sister when shit hit the fan. Then, I was kidnapped, and now I'm sitting in a police interrogation room being offered a chance to redeem myself by the hottest fucking agent, and rather than deciding what to do, I'm stuffing my face with Laffy Taffy and thinking inappropriate thoughts about Agent Cox and his chiseled jaw. His muscular arms. Gorgeous hazel eyes. Kissable lips. Tight perfect ass. I shake my head and scoff, I'm fucked when it comes to Agent Corey Cox but if I'm going to turn my life around, I need him.

Popping another candy into my mouth, I lean back in the uncomfortable metal chair, and mull over everything he offered. Instead of coming to a decision, I become angry when I think about how he spoke to me. To be honest, I'm fucking fuming right now. How dare he threaten me? Threaten the safety of Ave, fucking asshole.

Staring at the two-way mirror, I wonder if he's watching me. In case he is, I flip the bird toward the glass and stick my tongue out.

Standing up, I start pacing the room. My breathing becomes labored and my heart is racing, but it's not because of the decision before me, it's because of *him*, Agent Corey-fucking-Cox, and that I was beaten up recently.

Flopping back into the chair, I sigh as a slight throbbing begins between my thighs. I'm currently turned on by this sexy-as-fuck agent, what's up with that? How can I find him attractive when he holds my life in the palm of his hand? All I can think about is him bending me over this metal table and fucking the life out of me. *Seriously, Bay, focus.*

With a frustrated sigh, I lower my head to the table and wince at the contact. My face is a mess right now. I'm pretty sure I also have a cracked rib and I stink. The fucking assholes who took me messed with the wrong person, if they weren't already dead, I'd kill them myself.

The door opens again and my head lifts up to see a paramedic standing there. "Agent Cox sent me in to reassess you."

"I was assessed at the scene," I tell the lady.

"Won't hurt to get a second opinion," she says, walking into the room and placing her bag on the table.

"Fine," I huff, crossing my arms over my chest and wincing when my wrists rub against my shirt and I'm taken back to that room.

The rope cutting into my wrists.

The tight grip around my neck.

The sting in my cheek when they hit me.

She touches my shoulder and I flinch. "You don't seem fine," she sasses with a grin, reminding me of, well me.

"Fine," I concede, wiping at the corner of my eye, "I'm not fine. I hurt all over and I stink."

She steps over to me and stares at my face. "Looks like you went a few rounds with Mike Tyson."

"I feel like I went a few rounds with him AND Muhammad Ali."

"And you're still standing to tell the tale," she says. Taking my chin in her hand, she turns my head side to side, looking at my face. She scrunches up her nose. "You in any pain?"

"A little, but I'm a tough gal." She eyes me in that 'don't bullshit me' kind of way. "Fine, I'm exhausted and ready to collapse."

"Well, let's get you fixed up. You can chat with Agent Cox and then you can go on your merry way."

"Yeah, that's not gonna happen anytime soon."

She nods but doesn't say anything. She pulls out some medical supplies and gets to cleaning me up. Clearly, the first paramedic did a crappy job because the pile of used swabs is huge.

"I'll get you something to drink, and let Agent Cox know you are all cleaned up."

"Thanks," I tell her, and watch as she packs everything up and exits the room. Once again leaving me alone again with my dirty thoughts of Agent Cox.

The sound of the door opening startles me, seems I drifted off to sleep. The original officer enters again, and I deflate when I realize it's him. I'd much rather it had been Agent Cox, but I'm sure I will be seeing him again soon. Movement behind him catches my eye and I smile when I see it's Ave.

"Avie," I cry, pushing the chair back and standing up.

"BayBay," she blubbers, her eyes roaming over me.

Racing over to her, I wrap my arms around her and she returns the gesture. She squeezes me tightly, and it hurts like a bitch, but emotion overcomes me and together, we hug and cry. "I was so worried," she sniffles. "I've been going out of my mind with worry the last four days." Pulling back, she gently grips my cheeks in her palms. "Are you okay?"

"Yeah, I'm fine," I whisper, my voice is anything but and it totally gives me away.

Ave stares at me. "Wanna try again?"

"You know me too well."

Her face deflates. "I used to know you too well. Now, not so much," she says, pulling me over to the chairs. She sits down but I don't. She stares up at me, her face etched with fear and anger. "You need to start talking, Bay!"

"Always the responsible one," I grumble, getting pissed she's playing mother hen right now. Once again, perfect Avery to the rescue.

"Bay," she pleads. "What happened?"

"Long story." I nonchalantly reply.

"Bay," she warns. The tone in her voice affects me in a way I haven't felt since we were little.

"Fine, I'll tell you, but first, I need you to listen to everything I have to say."

Her face pales and I hate I'm putting her through this. "I'm not going to like this, am I?" she asks.

Shaking my head, I confirm, "Probably not…" I take a deep breath, wincing at the tightness in my ribs. "…but, Avery, I need to do this. I need to make amends for my actions. I need to do this for Kye."

"Who is Kye, Bay?"

My eyes well up again, they're a mixture of angry, sad, and confused tears. "I thought he was 'the one' and because of my actions, I thought he died. It should have been me, but he protected me. Like I told you at the hospital, I tried to walk away after that, but I was in too deep. Way too deep." I bite my lip and stare at her. "But it was all a farce, he tricked me and lied. Avie, this is my chance to put things right. This is my chance to make up for his death, well, for the death of, I don't even know his name." As I say this, I start to doubt if he was 'the one' and I have so many questions: who was I with? Kye or his doppelgänger? Why did he do this to me? How could I fall for his lies? "For once, I want to do the right thing."

"I'm so proud of you, BayBay." Her words shock me. "And that's the honest truth. Last week, I was broken up and hurt over your actions, and now, I could not be prouder of you." She squeezes my hand. "This the Bay I know and love. You are taking charge of your life. You are owning your mistakes and you are trying to put things right." I see nothing but happiness and pride in her face and it confirms I'm making the right decision. "Okay, now, tell me the plan that I'm not going to like."

Taking a seat next to her, I stare at my sister. "Well, when the agents found me, River and Smallie were being dick-heads, as usual. They were waiting for orders from Kye—"

"You said Kye was dead."

"Spoiler alert, he's not. Cox just informed me he's alive and well. Apparently, the person I saw die wasn't him."

"This is like something from a movie."

"Tell me about it. Anyway, when you were attacked, they were coming to get me to take me to him, but when that went to shit, the plan changed. Once they got me, it went to shit again because I was rescued before the supposedly dead Kye turned up. In the process, River and Smallie were killed, which are all good things because for one, they were fuckers, and two, it led me to here and the redeeming of me."

"Okay, so what's the part I'm not going to like?"

"Cox—"

"Who's Cox?" she asks.

"Some agent," *a sexy as hell agent* "who needs my help to bring down Kye and his drug ring."

"Bay," she pleads, "I don't like this."

"Can't say I'm a fan either, but I need to do this, Avie. This is my chance to make amends for my actions and redeem myself. Also, my time served will be reduced, and I ain't gonna let that asshole get away with what he did to me. He needs to pay for that."

"Can't you just do jail like a normal person?"

"Nope, not my style," I nonchalantly say with a shrug.

"Why any jail time at all, if you're helping them?"

"The great gnome arrest from when I was twenty."

"Fucking gnomes," she scoffs and I laugh.

"Fucking gnomes," I agree. "Anyway, helping will reduce my time to twelve months rather than two years."

"Isn't there another way?"

Shaking my head, I reply, "No, Ave, there isn't."

"Is it wrong that right now I want Bitchy Baylor to appear, and for you to tell everyone to go fuck themselves or to fuck off?"

"Ohh, she did," Agent Cox says as he reenters the room. "Multiple times."

CHAPTER 3

Corey

BOTH OF THEM turn to face me.

"Fuck, you again," Baylor says, while at the same time her sister asks, "Who the hell are you?"

"Wow, for twin sisters you're different, yet the same," I say, walking over to Avery, I stretch out my hand, "Agent Corey Cox, it's a pleasure to meet you, Ms. Evans."

She shakes my hand but eyes me suspiciously.

"So you're the one with this plan for my sister." She air quotes plan and stares intently at me, her glare isn't as intimidating as her sister's, but it's still frightening. "What will you do to guarantee her safety?"

"I can't one-hundred-percent—"

"Then no, my sister will not be doing this."

"Ave," Baylor intrudes, "I have to do this. It's either this or jail. I really don't have a choice."

"Why?" her sister pleads.

"Because I need answers. I need to know why Kye did what he did, but more importantly, I want to bring the asshole down. No one fucks me over like that."

A laugh escapes my lips, causing Baylor to turn her head toward me, scowling, and raising her eyebrows defiantly. "What the fuck is so funny, asshole?"

"Watch your mouth, Baylor," she huffs and crosses her arms and winces a little but my eyes are locked on her pushed-up tits. She clears her throat and I lift my gaze to hers. "You constantly surprise me and that's exactly why you are the perfect person for this assignment. Even if you are a pain in my ass."

"Am not," she sasses back.

Shaking my head, I take a seat across them and look toward her sister. "Avery, I will do everything I can to ensure Baylor gets through this safely."

"But—" she protests, but Baylor interrupts her.

"Avie, I'll be fine," Baylor confidently says, reaching out to squeeze her sister's hand, "I can hold my ground with the best of them, besides I'm Bitchy Baylor, I've got this."

"No, you're my BayBay and I worry. I know you're strong but you're my sister, my twinsie. I don't want to lose you. I know you are a tough b-i-t-c-h, but—"

"Did you just spell bitch?" Baylor questions her sister.

Avery nonchalantly shrugs. "Yeah, and?"

"You are something else, Avie. Like seriously, how are we twins? We are—"

"Baylor, focus," Avery snaps. "Please don't do this. Choose time in jail. It's safer. I'll hire you a great lawyer, I'll do everything I can to help you. I just can't lose you, Bay."

"Avie, I choose Cox," she looks to me, and her words affect me in a way they shouldn't, "and his plan. I want do this." She looks me dead in the eye, "I'm one-hundred-percent in."

"Are you sure about this, Bay?" her sister questions again, clearly uneasy with her sister's decision. She's worried about her sister's safety and I get it, but I need Baylor to do this.

"Yeah, I'm sure." She looks back at her sister and smiles, but it's forced. Underneath her tough girl front, she's scared and she should be, this will not be a walk in the park. If I'm honest, there's a huge chance this will go tits up and Baylor's life could be in jeopardy, but it's a risk that needs to be taken, and I will do my darnedest to keep her safe and get my man. "I'll be fine, Avie. Promise." They hug each other and the moment between them reminds me of my brother, Hunter, and me, well before his death that is.

Avery's eyes widen and she pulls away from Baylor, "Ohh, candy," she says, reaching over to grab one from the box I left for Baylor, but before she can grab one, Baylor slaps her hand away.

"Mine," she growls at her sister, but what surprises me is she's staring at me as she says this and not at her sister.

"Wow, living up to your name of Bitchy Baylor right now." She shakes her head. "I forgot how possessive you get of your grape Laffy Taffy."

"See, you do know me…and you just swore," Bay sasses at her sister. Avery sticks her tongue out in that affectionate, sisterly way. "And yes, you may have one. Only cause you said bitchy." She emphasizes the word one. Avery leans over and grabs two candies, garnering a growl from the Laffy Taffy warden.

Baylor grabs one herself and pops the treat into her mouth, "So what's the plan, Stan?"

"Don't ever call me that again," I snap.

Baylor leans into her sister. "This one has a stick up his ass," she not-so-quietly whispers.

"I heard that."

"You were meant to. You really need to take a chill pill or get laid…maybe even both."

"Baylor," her sister warns, "Be nice. You just agreed to help Agent Cox."

"He needs me more than I need him," she snaps at her sister.

"Baylor, if you like, I can call Hall and Oats," Avery giggles at this, "and have you transferred over to the holding cell. My offer will be off the table and you can serve out your full sentence. It's no skin off my nose." I really hope she doesn't call my bluff because she really is my last hope. "The decision is yours, but believe me, my offer is better than what you are currently facing." I flick open the file and pretend to read but I know this file front to back. "You are facing charges for felony distribution, possession, and I'm sure I can find a few traffic infringements to add to the list too."

"Get fucked, asshole."

"Watch it. The way I see it, Baylor, you help me, or get used to the color orange for the next few years. What will it be?"

"I like you," Avery says, staring directly at me. She turns her attention back to her sister. "Baylor, I you need to listen to him. Tame your inner beast for once in your life."

"Harsh much?" Baylor snaps at her sister.

I hold back a laugh; I like this one too. For twins, Baylor and Avery Evans are total opposites but there are also many similarities, including their looks. If you didn't know better, it would be easy to mistake one for the other. I can see why River and Smallie thought Avery was Baylor.

"Baylor, seriously," Avery lashes out at her sister, no longer is she calm, cool, and collected. Her fears over her sister are surfacing and she's laying it all out in the table for Baylor. "Pull your head out of your ass. For once in your life, play nice and listen. You are literally being handed the best lifeline anyone could ask for, and you're going to piss it all away if you keep this up. Just stop being Bitchy Baylor and be Benevolent Baylor. Please, Bay," she begs, "do the right thing, if not, you will end up in prison for a long time, or worse...dead."

Baylor stares in disbelief at her sister, I don't think Avery has ever spoken to her like this before. Baylor is taken aback by the forceful nature of her sister just now, but I'm confident that Baylor can do this. Sure, she plays tough, but from my observations, underneath her bitchy exterior is a person with a heart who wants to do the right thing.

She puts on a front, I know because her actions and personality remind me so much of Hunter. He, too, was in a similar predicament, but unfortunately for him, he didn't have someone watching his back and he lost his life. He's the reason I became an agent. He's the reason I want to help Baylor, because the similarities of their situation mirror one another, and I will not lose someone in that manner again.

Her shoulders lower and she reaches over to take her sister's hand again. "Ave, I'm going to do this. I already agreed. I know I need to do it. I don't have any other choice, plus as I said before, I'll get answers. But most of all, I need, no, I want to redeem myself." *BINGO, I knew there was a soft side to this woman,* I think to myself, but she shocks me when she quietly adds, "I don't like the person I've become, Avie. I want to be more like you. I want people to want to be around me. I want someone to love me like Flynn loves you. I want a friend who will drop anything to be there for me like Cress does for you. I want to start living life rather than just coasting through."

"Ohh, Bay," Avery cries. "I'm so proud of you right now."

The moment between the sisters is heartwarming but time is of the essence right now. "Sorry to break up this Hall-mark moment, ladies, but we need to get this in motion. Baylor needs to get out of here so we can bring this all crashing down."

Baylor looks to me and confidently says, "Let's do this."

CHAPTER 4

Baylor

AVE LEFT and I spent the next few hours formulating the plan with Agent Cox and his superior. There was so much paperwork. I lost count of how many times I was threatened if I took off or betrayed him. Like I could go anywhere, he took my passport and I have no clue how to go underground as they say.

He's so anal with everything—the complete opposite of me—ensuring all the I's are dotted and the T's are crossed. I've never met someone as straitlaced as him... and Anal Avery is my sister. He sees everything as black and white, there's no gray or in between. And rules, fuck me sideways. Him and his rules are going to drive me fucking nuts. If he keeps pushing me, I'll show him my claws like the kitten he keeps referring to me as. Little does he know, I'm not a kitten, I'm a fucking lion. I'm the queen of the jungle and I'm going to bring him, Kye, and this case, to their knees.

Thankfully I can still live at the apartment with Ave, but I will be suggesting she stay with Flynn more often than not. I don't want her to get hurt again. I keep playing the image of stepping out of the elevator and seeing River and Smallie standing above her limp, lifeless body and the events that unfolded after…

…*I've had this feeling of being watched the last few days, but it's clearly my mind playing tricks on me because no one is there. Hell, I swore I saw Kye the other day when I was doing a drop-off for Creed. Stepping into the elevator, I press the button for my floor; this is the slowest elevator in the history of elevators. The doors open and when I step out, I see River and Smallie and wonder what they're doing here. Then, I see Ave on the ground and a sinking feeling develops in the pit of my stomach. Smallie lifts his leg back and kicks Ave like she's a football. My eyes widen and I'm frozen, but then, instinct kicks in and I shake my head and race out of the elevator.*

"Avie!" I scream, and this causes their heads to snap up.

They look at me stunned, and then, one of them growls, "Fuck." Smallie kicks her again and from the force, her head connects with the doorframe and I watch as she loses consciousness.

"What the fuck, guys?"

"We thought she was you," River says, looking agitated and guilty.

"Why are you here?"

"The boss wants what's his."

"And what's that?"

But before he can answer, our nosey next-door neighbor exits his apartment. "What's going on?" he asks, looking between the three of us, he hasn't noticed Ave yet. Needing to cause a distrac-

tion and get the guys out of here, I shout, "Call 911," and race over to Ave.

"Fucking bitch," one of them yells, as they make a beeline for the emergency stairwell.

"Ohh, Baylor," I cry, keeping up the ruse that it's me who has been assaulted.

"Emergency services are on their way," the neighbor says, but I stare at Ave and hope that she'll be okay as I quietly whisper, "Shit, shit, shit. This is all my fault. "

"Avery," the neighbor says, pulling me out of my thoughts.

"Yes," I answer, reaffirming that I'm Avery.

"Can I get you anything?"

Shaking my head, I stare down at Ave and take her hand in mind. "Please be okay," I whisper.

The elevator doors open and the paramedics walk over to us. They shuffle me out of the way and get to work on Ave/me. She's loaded onto the stretcher and they hand me her bag. I follow after them and climb in with her. We pull up at Western General, where she's whisked away and I'm escorted to the waiting area in the ER.

Taking a seat, I stare at the two bags on my lap. My purple Prada and Ave's simple black tote; even our bags are different. Her phone rings but I don't answer, I just stare at the purses on my lap. Her phone pings that a voicemail has been left. Without thinking, I reach in and grab her phone. I see she has a missed call from Flynn.

"Ms. Evans?" a nurse asks.

Lifting my head, I look up at her. "Yes,"

"Your sister is being taken to X-ray. We will know more soon."

Nodding my head, I watch her walk away. That should be me in there. Her phone pings again, so I look down at the screen and it's a text from Cressida. Ignoring that, I click on Flynn's name, he needs to be here for Ave. He picks up immediately, "Ave, babe—"

He thinks I'm her and before I can stop myself, I cry, "Flynn... it's Bay."

"What's wrong? Where are you?" His voice is etched with worry and jealousy courses though me. No one would worry or care for me like that.

"I'm at Western General," I tell him.

"I'm on my way."

"Hurry."

Hanging up from Flynn, I go back to staring the bags on my lap. Movement in the corner of my eye causes me to lift my head, and I see the nurse from before walking over to me with two officers. "Ms. Evans, I'm Officer Cooper and this here is my partner, Officer Devon."

I nod my head, "Hi," I mumble, gripping the strap of my bag tighter.

"Can you tell us what happened tonight?"

"It's all jumbled but I got home and two guys were standing over her. They were shocked to see me."

"Do you think they were after you and not your sister?" The officer's question shocks me but at the same time, I was also

expecting it. Everyone knows Avery Evans is a saint and I'm not, so it's unsurprising they would ask that. I know this is the time to admit that it's Ave in there, but the lies continue to fall from my mouth.

"I...I don't know," I lie, because they were one-hundred-percent after me. Avery is innocent in all of this. Avery is always innocent and it's always me in trouble. I will myself to tell the truth. To say, "There's been a mistake, I'm Baylor, it's Avery in there. They were after me. I'm the bitch here." But before I can confess, Flynn enters the ER. My heart stops because I know I'm about to be caught. He's her boyfriend, he will know I'm not Ave but I don't correct them.

Taking a deep breath, I close my eyes, but when I open them, my gaze lands on him; I just can't do it. I live up to my 'Bitchy Baylor' name and continue the ruse that I'm Avery Evans. "Flynn," I cry, wrapping my arms around his waist and snuggling into him. I breakdown and weep into his chest. He wraps his arms around me, hugging me tight. I feel safe in his arms. It's nice to be held and wanted and loved, even if the person doing all of that thinks I'm someone else.

I know what I'm doing is wrong, but I can't stop myself...and I don't care a bit it's all a farce.

Tears fall down my cheeks. I don't know if I'm crying because I'll never have a love like this, or if I'm crying because my sister, my number one cheerleader, is in there because of me and my actions.

His embrace tightens and he soothingly whispers, 'Shhhh' over and over, reminding me so much of Ave.

Guilt sets in but when Flynn says, "Avery here is my girl-friend." It snaps my attention back to the present. This is when I need to come clean, but I like being someone's girlfriend again. I haven't had that since Kye and even if just for tonight, I can be happy and loved, then I'm going to take it.

The officers look at me, waiting for confirmation that Flynn is my boyfriend, so I nod in agreement. Flynn is Avery's boyfriend so that's not a lie. The only lie is I'm Baylor and not Avery.

The officer addresses Flynn, "Baylor was attacked by two unknown assailants, at the apartment she shares with her sister earlier this evening. Avery, here, interrupted them and probably saved her sister."

"I was so scared, baby," I say, snuggling into Flynn's side. Surprising myself how easy it is right now to pretend to be Ave.

Flynn places a kiss on my head. "Babe, I'm so glad you weren't home when it happened. Do you know who they were?"

I shake my head, and another lie slips through my lips. "No, I've never seen them before."

"Are they the guys from the other day?" he asks me. I have no idea what he's going on about. He eyes me suspiciously and then adds, "You mentioned two guys the other night?

"I...I don't know. Everything's all so fuzzy." Pulling away from him, I sit down and cover my face with my hands. This is getting out of control, I need to confess but when Flynn says, "What shit has your sister gotten into?" my blood boils. Of course he thinks this is all my fault. I look at him and snarl, "Who says it's her fault?"

"I didn't say that, I—" Before he can defend himself, a doctor walks over to us, Flynn stands up to greet him. I sit and watch them, after giving permission for Dr. Clay to speak freely, he gives us an update on me slash Ave.

"Avery, Baylor has a concussion and a laceration to her left cheek that needed five stitches, but luckily, no broken facial bones. She has three cracked ribs and a nasty bump on the back of her head. Her face and torso are bruised, likely from being kicked. She was also shocked with a Taser. There's two red barb welts on the side of her abdomen. All things considered, she's in okay shape." Dr. Clay adds, *"She's still unconscious and we will continue to monitor her until she wakes up."*

Rapidly blinking I process his words, but everything is all jumbled. Hearing the extent of her injuries concerns me. "Will...will she be okay?"

"Until she regains consciousness, we won't know about her mental state but physically, yes, she'll recover from the injuries sustained."

"Can I see her?"

Dr. Clay nods his head. "Of course. Come with me. Flynn, technically, you cannot see her."

"No, I understand," he says before turning to me. "You go see your sister and I'll see about getting her transferred to a room upstairs."

Wrapping my arms around him, I kiss him. I know I shouldn't, but I close my eyes and press my lips to his. He's stiff, it's like he knows I'm not her but he's too nice to say anything.

Pulling away, I follow Dr. Clay, leaving Flynn behind.

Taking a seat beside Ave, I stare down at her. My eyes well with tears. Taking her hand in mine, I squeeze. "Please wake up. I'm so sorry, twinsie. Please wake up for me."

Seeing her lying there changed something inside of me. Yes, it still took me some time to come clean, well, for Cressida to out me, but I feel remorseful for what I had caused, and after chatting with Ave once she woke up, I knew it was time to make a few changes in my life. I want to be someone she's proud of again. I wanted to be her BayBay.

Another deciding factor in turning my life around was when River and Smallie took me from the hospital. After being tortured for a few days, I was more than determined to change; this wasn't the life I wanted anymore and I definitely don't want to be tortured again. I never expected my chance to reform come in the form of a straitlaced sexy agent with an offer right out of the movies, but here we are. I'm about to go undercover to help him bring down a major drug ring that is run by my presumably dead boyfriend. *Tarantino couldn't write this shit*, I think to myself, as I walk toward the warehouse.

My second chance starts now, and I'm not going to let them down. With my hand on the doorknob, I push it open and enter.

It's go time.

It's showtime!

CHAPTER 5
Baylor

STEPPING INSIDE THE WAREHOUSE, I thought I was prepared to see him. I'd seen the surveillance photo of Kye, but there was still a part of me that thought Cox was fucking with me. But he wasn't because standing before me, alive and breathing, is Kye Vlahos.

My breath hitches. "You...you're...you're dead," I stammer, blinking rapidly. My eyes lock on the alive and breathing Kye Vlahos. Cox told me I needed to act surprised when I saw Kye for the first time, but I guarantee you, I'm not acting right now.

"Surprise, Sugar. Daddy's home," he says, stretching out his arms, smiling at me.

"H...how? W...what? How?" I stutter.

"I think we need to talk, Sugar," he says, walking over to me. My rapidly blinking eyes are locked on him. He cups my cheek with his palm, and my breath hitches again when his hand connects with my skin. Lifting my hand, I cover his with mine, leaning into it. Squeezing. Breathing him in.

"You're really here?" I whisper.

"In the flesh, Sugar." His voice is deeper than I remember but he looks exactly the same, except his hair is a little longer. "What did they do to you?" he whispers, gently running his thumb across my bruised cheekbone.

"Who?"

"Smallie and River."

"It doesn't matter what they did. How are you alive?"

"Yes, it fucking matters," he snarls. "No one touches what's mine." The vehemence in his voice is frightening. I don't remember him ever speaking like this before. "If they weren't already dead, I'd kill them myself."

Staring at him, I process his words and actions. He's being so nice to me. It's as if he does love me, but if he did, why did he let me think he was dead? Looking directly into his eyes, I glare at him. "If I meant so much to you," I snap, "you wouldn't have let me think you were dead these last few months." I pull his hand off my face and throw it to the side. I step back and spin around, shaking my head.

Turning back to face him, my eyes well with tears when the emotion I felt at losing him hits me with the force of a Category 5 hurricane, "Why, Kye? Why?" I cry, "Why did you make me think you were dead? I loved you. I thought you loved me too."

"It's complicated," he nonchalantly replies, slipping his hands into his jean pockets, rocking on his feet, as if he doesn't have a care in the world. As if he didn't just reappear from the dead.

"Don't give me that shit!" I yell, anger building at how calm and cool he's acting right now. "How dare you treat me like that!"

"Sugar," he interrupts.

"Don't fucking Sugar me. I want answers, Kye, and I want them now."

"Calm your tits, woman. I'm trying to explain but you're going all psycho bitch on me right now."

"Did you just, A. Tell me to calm my fucking tits, and B. Call me psycho fucking bitch? YOU," I point at him, "are the fucking asshole, dickwad cunt. You made me think you were dead." My eyes well up with tears. "I cried for you. My heart broke for you and all along, you were fucking alive."

"I know. I'm sorry I did that but if you let me explain..."

"You died, Kye. I saw it," I cry, tears are pouring down my face now. I thought I was going to be okay with his deceit, but seeing him alive and breathing, it cuts me that he didn't confide in me. "Why?"

"Sugar," he says, cupping my cheeks in his palms, "I had to get the feds off my ass and take care of a few family matters. I didn't want you to get caught up in this until it was safe."

"Why do they care about us? We are nothing. Nobodies."

"Baylor, Sugar. I'm Kye-fucking-Vlahos, head of the Vlahos family. Since the recent demise of my father, mother, sister, and uncles, the family empire is mine." He pauses. "Mine."

My eyes widen, seems Cox left out a major detail, but then it hits me, he didn't know this. "What?"

"It was all planned, Sugar. I took out Father and his brothers, and no one suspected a fucking thing. Mother and sister were collateral, their deaths earlier today were unfortunate, but now, now I'm back where I belong."

"And where's that? Hell?"

He laughs at me, "No, in the seat at the head of the Vlahos family, where I rightfully belong. And Bay, Sugar, I want you by my side every step of the way from now on. What do you say, Sugar? Will you reign as my queen?"

CHAPTER 6

Corey

WATCHING Baylor walk out of the room just now was harder than I anticipated. I've sent many people undercover, but this woman, she's affected me in a way like never before.

A knock at the door garners my attention, and I look up to see Hall standing in the doorway. "Saw Baylor leave, wanted to check that your balls are still attached."

"My balls are safe, thanks for your concern."

"Why the long face then?

"I'm concerned," I tell him, rapping my fingers repeatedly on the file before me.

"Concerned about what?" he asks, walking into the room and taking the seat Baylor just vacated.

"This case."

"Having second thoughts about using such a wild card?"

"I'm not concerned about sending her in, I'm worried about what could happen to her. Kye Vlahos and his associates are crazy motherfuckers. I can normally see an endgame, but not this time."

"Lay it all out for me then, maybe you need an outsider's view."

"Okay, Kye fakes his death, and while he's 'dead', his family members all die in non-suspicious ways, which makes them suspicious. Then he reappears from the dead and takes the seat at the head of the family. What is he up to? A source tells me he's been following Baylor and then two of his men take her and rough her up. Why did they do that? There are too many crazy pieces, and I can't make them all fit together."

"Can't believe I'm saying this but by sending Baylor in, you're on the right track. Crazy plus crazy equals answers." We both laugh. "Look, give her time, she's been gone for ten fucking minutes."

"Yeah, I guess so."

"I still think she's a wild card and you are a crazy fucker for using her, but with the elements you just laid out, seems like she's exactly what you need to crack this case wide open... as long as she sticks to the plan and the rules." He stands up and slaps the folder before me. "Go home, get some sleep. Tomorrow's a new day." With that, he walks out, leaving me alone.

Leaning back in my chair, I link my fingers behind my head, and think back to earlier this evening when I laid out the rules to Baylor...

…"*Are you listening, Ms. Evans?*"

"*No, I'm just sitting here staring at your lips moving, thinking about cocktails and eating nachos while being on a beach in Mexico. Of course, I'm listening.*"

"*Well, what did I just say?*"

"*Ummm…*"

"*Exactly my point. You need to pay attention. Your life is on the line here, do you want to end up dead?*"

"*No one would care if I did die.*"

"*Your sister would.*"

"*Leave Ave out of this,*" she snarls, the glint in her eye darkening at the mention of her sister.

"*Well, focus, and I won't bring her up again but, Ms. Evans, this is serious. If it goes wrong, I can't guarantee your safety… and I really don't want to have to tell your sister you didn't make it. For a small thing, she's feisty.*"

"*She gets that from me.*"

"*No shit,*" I say, "*Now, can we get back to this?*"

"*Fine,*" she huffs, crossing her arms across her chest. She winces slightly. "*Can you start again, please?*"

"*Fine,*" I throw her words back at her. "*Once you leave here, you'll be on your own in the field, but we will be listening in via this,*" I lift up a phone, "*hidden in the case is a microphone that will transmit to us twenty-four seven. Once a week, I'll stop by the apartment at an agreed time, and we can discuss the plan forward. I'll be posing as a contractor you and Avery are using for upgrades on the apartment.*"

"Like you've done a day of fucking hard labor in your life."

"You know nothing about me, Kitten." She growls but I ignore her. "As I was saying, we will meet up once a week, unless you make contact to meet earlier. You can reach me using this," I hand her a burner phone, "keep it at home at all times. Kye and his men cannot see or get access to this."

"Gotcha. What specifically do you need?"

"Anything and everything." I laugh, running my finger through my hair. "Names, dates, times, schedules, anything you think will be beneficial in bringing him down."

She nods her head. "Can I ask a question?"

"Of course."

"Do you really think I can do this?"

"I do. I think you can do anything you put your mind to. I think you hide behind this snarky bitchy front because you're scared."

"I'm not scared," she snaps, "I'm..."

"You're what?" I ask, my voice laced with concern. This is the first time Baylor has shown any emotion, other than sassiness. If she's one bit hesitant, I can't in good conscience allow her to do this.

"I...I don't know who I am or what I want in life. Ave knew she wanted to be a teacher since forever, she knows who she is. I've never found who I am and it feels like everyone compares me to her." She pauses and smiles. "She really is the best. Ave doesn't have a mean bone in her body and then there's me. Crazy wild me, marching to the beat of my own drum and not caring about consequences. You know, the first time in my life that I felt anything was when I started working with, well I guess, for Kye.

They treated me with respect, they didn't compare me to Saint Avery but I guarantee you, if they met her, they would. Everyone loves her."

"Stop! I interrupt her, and the use of her first name startles her. Standing up, I walk around the table and lean against the edge next to her. She lifts her gaze to me. "I see you, Baylor, and I see a strong confident woman who just needs someone to believe in her. And guess what?"

"What?" she timidly asks, her eyes locked on mine.

They are filled with vulnerability but also fire, my little fire-cracker is still in there. She's scared of what lies ahead and she should be, but I won't let anything happen to her. Poking myself in the chest, "Me," I honestly tell her, "I believe in you."

Her eyes widen at my response, her mouth opens and closes a few times and then my sassy little kitten is back. "You're just saying that because you need me."

Shaking my head, I laugh. "Yes, I need you but, Ms. Evans, do you really think if I didn't believe in you, I'd send you in there?" Standing up, I walk around the desk and lean against the timber. "You are my winning piece."

"So I'm just a pawn in your game?" She pauses. "It's me who's risking everything here."

"Is my kitten afraid of a challenge?"

"I didn't say that," she sassily snaps back at me.

"But you didn't deny it either, Ms. Evans."

"You are infuriating, you know that?" I shrug at her. "I was merely pointing out that I'm the pawn in this."

"Ms. Evans, a lot of people may have underestimated you in the past but believe me when I say this, if anyone can bring down Kye Vlahos, it will be you."

We silently stare at one another, processing the words just spoken. Something passes between us. We've turned a corner in our relationship and for the first time since I formulated this plan, I think that we can actually do this. This blonde-haired, blue-eyed woman is going to bring down the Vlahos family and they won't see her coming.

"Thank you," she whispers, "for believing in me. I won't let you down." Taking a deep breath, she stands . "I guess it's time to get this show on the road."

"Yep," I say, letting the P pop.

She walks toward the door but before she opens it, she turns to face me. "Thank you, Corey. For the pep talk, even if I think you're full of fucking shit."

Before I can reply, she turns the handle and walks out of my office…

…My phone pings with a text. Picking it up, I read the message. It says two words *She's in.*

After she left here, I had her followed to make sure she didn't try and take off. I was positive she wouldn't run, but there was also a part of me that thought she might.

Picking up the photo of her we have in the file, I stare at it. At her. "It's all up to you now, Baylor," I whisper to the photo.

Placing the image back into the file, I pack up my things and head home.

I'm in my kitchen pacing, before I wear a hole in the tiles, I change into some sweats, pull on my sneakers, and go for a run. I bring up Spotify and Rammstein begins playing as I exit my building. I head toward the Lakefront Path and run along Lake Michigan. A quick ten-mile run is just what I need to clear my head, because right now, Baylor Evans is on my mind and I need to focus, especially if I'm going to get her through this alive.

CHAPTER 7
Baylor

IT'S BEEN seven days since I made my deal with Cox, and I'm no closer to getting anything from Kye. He's keeping me at an arm's length but at the same time, he tells me he wants me by his side as his queen. It feels like he's testing me, I don't know why he's doubting me, I've never betrayed him, or given him any reason not to trust me...unlike him.

I'm at the warehouse, waiting for Kye and Creed to return. That Creed guy is seriously unhinged. He keeps talking about Cressida and her new beau and how he hates him, blah, blah, blah. I tune out when he talks, but the last few times he's said some really sinister things about Cressida. Look, I'm not her number one fan but seriously, the way he talks about his baby momma, it's disgusting.

What's even more shocking, he brought Lexi here yesterday. Who does that? Who brings their kid to a place like this? She's cute for being Cressida's kid, not that I'd ever admit it out loud. It's a shame her dad is a dick and her mom is such a bitch. Her mom, Cressida Bayliss, is Avie's best friend so she's always at the apartment but lately, not so much, which is fine by me.

Gaga comes on and I start humming along to "Born this Way" when there's a commotion outside. The door swings open, and Creed and Kye enter. Kye is holding his side and leaning on Creed for support. "Kye," I shout. Jumping up, I race over to them. "What happened?"

"Fuckers got one up on me."

"Are you hurt?" I ask, placing my hand over his.

"Just a small stab wound," he says through clenched teeth, as Creed lowers him to the sofa.

"You need to go to the hospital," I say, crouching down next to him. He's sweating and looks pale. I'm no doctor but he looks like he's dying.

"Nah," he shakes his head, "the doc is on her way."

I stare at him, about to say something, when the door opens and I hear heels clicking across the cement floor. Looking over my shoulder, I see a brunette with fake tits and a dress that's painted on walking toward us. Her eyes roam over Kye and a ragey, stabby feeling begin to fester and flow through my veins.

"Kye, darling," she singsongs, her voice grating on my nerves. "What happened?"

"I got stabbed," he replies.

She leans down and kisses him, he turns his head—at the last minute—and her lips land at the corner of his mouth. A growl forms in the back of my throat seeing this.

Both of them turn their heads to look at me. "What?" I snarl.

"You jealous, Sugar?" Kye says, placing his hand on the bitch's ass, squeezing, licking his lips like a fucking pig.

Slapping his hand off her ass, I stand up and stalk away. He laughs at my retreating form and it pisses me off.

Storming down the hallway, I enter Kye's bedroom and slam the door behind me. Flopping back onto the bed, I sigh. Then I quickly stand up and tear the sheets off. He probably fucked her on these sheets. I don't know why I'm acting like this. I don't love him anymore, but the thought of him with someone else enrages me.

Grabbing the sheets, I open the door and throw them into the hallway before slamming the door shut again. Walking back into the room, I sit on the end of the bed and kick off my purple heels. Breathing rapidly, I fall back onto the mattress and stare up at the ceiling.

My outburst just now is confusing to me. I don't care for him in that way, but when I saw him with *her*, I became jealous. I'm not a jealous person. Resting my arm over my eyes, I sigh. I don't think I can do this. My emotions are all over the place and if I'm not careful, I'm gonna end up dead.

Why is doing the right thing so hard?

Closing my eyes, I drift off to sleep, only to be woken when there's a banging on the door. "Baylor, Bossman wants you!" Creed shouts through the door.

"Tell him to fuck off!" I shout back.

"Your funeral," he says.

"Whatever," I mumble, lifting my arm, I rest it on my forehead and exhale deeply. That fear of not being able to do this rears its ugly head again. "I can't do this," I whisper, my eyes welling with tears.

The door opens and Kye walks in.

Lifting my head, I wipe my eyes and see a shirtless Kye standing there, a bandage around his waist, color back in his cheeks. We stare at one another, neither one of us speaking.

"Did you fuck her?" I snarl, breaking the silence.

Sitting up, I pull my feet onto the edge of the mattress and wrap my arms around my legs, resting my chin on my knees. I look down at my toes, wriggling them. The purple polish sparkles in the dim bedroom light.

"Not today," he replies, walking farther into the room.

"So, you have before?" I snap, lifting my gaze to his. Staring at him, I notice his eyes are locked on me.

"Yeah," he says, reaching out, he goes to cup my cheek but I slap his hand away.

"Well, go and fuck her now. She can be your fucking queen, since I mean so little to you." I'm shocked at the anger coming from me right now. I don't want him in that way. I don't want him in any way. I just want to bring him and his lying, deceiving, non-dead ass down.

"Bay, Sugar," he coos, squatting in front of me, he places his hands on my knees, "She's nothing to me." When I continue to stare at my toes, he lifts his hand and places it under my chin, lifting my gaze to his. "You're my queen, Sugar. It's you I want by my side, not her."

I believe him, I don't want to but I do. I nod my head in agreement. Kye smiles at me, and for a brief moment, the love I used to have for him simmers below the surface. He leans forward, threads his fingers into my hair, and presses his lips to mine. We fall back to the mattress and kiss, just like we used to. I close my eyes and give myself over to Kye and the kiss, hooking my leg around his back. What surprises me is that behind my closed eyes, I see Corey-fucking-Cox. I groan in shock, which Kye takes it as I'm enjoying this. He lifts his hand and cups my breast, pinching my nipple through my shirt and bra. I moan again but this time, it's a pleasurable one. I'm still picturing Corey as I give myself over to the pleasure coursing through me.

Wrapping my arms around his neck, I deepen the kiss and pull him into me. He hisses in pain, which pulls me out of my lust induced state. I suddenly start remembering why he got stabbed earlier and more importantly, I'm kissing Kye; not Corey. *What the fuck is wrong with me?*

Gently, I push him off me. "Kye, babe, you're hurt."

"I'm fine. Doc stitched me up."

At the mention of *her*, my anger returns, and this time when I push, he rolls off me. I stand up, turn around, and stare down at him. "We need a new doctor," I spit at him before spinning on my heel and walking into the bathroom, slamming the door behind me. Leaning my hands on the vanity edge, I stare at my reflection and shake my head. *What have I gotten myself into?*

The door opens. I look up and in the reflection of the mirror, I see Kye staring at me. He doesn't say anything; it's unnerving. "What?" I snap.

"Wanna talk about your jealousy?" He crosses his arms and leans against the doorframe. I silently watch him in the mirror and let out a frustrated sigh.

Turning to face him, I lean against the vanity, crossing my legs and arms, mimicking his stance.

"I presumed that you fucked others when you were 'dead' but seeing it, it…"

"It what?"

"It didn't piss me off and that pissed me off."

"So you're pissed off that you're not pissed?"

"Pretty much. It makes no sense." I look to my feet, wriggling my toes in the fluffy floor mat for something to focus on that isn't Kye.

"Do you care if I fuck Monica now?"

Lifting my head, I stare at him and shake my head from side to side. "No, I don't." I pause, "How can I be your queen if I don't care that you fuck her or anyone else?"

He steps over to me and rests his hands on my hips, "I chose you to be my queen because you are one badass bitch. You hold your ground. You don't cower to anyone. You command respect from my men but most all, you have my back. Do I want you in my bed? Fuck yes, I remember how good it was with you, but am I going to turn you away because you don't want that? Hell fucking no. Pussy is pussy—"

"Charming," I interrupt and smack his shoulder.

"Dick is dick too."

"Touché," I reply.

"Baylor, what do you want?"

Staring at him, I bite my bottom lip and think about what I want. "I want to be by your side as your queen, but right now, I can't be in your bed. I'm still hurt over you letting me think you were dead. And I'm still really pissed off at you sending Smallie and River to get me."

"They went off the grid, I still don't know what happened there."

"Creed happened. He tried to fuck you over. I guarantee it. That guy is a loose cannon, but getting back to us, fuck who you want, but I don't want to see or hear it. If and when I'm ready to be with you, I'll let you know."

"And that there is why you are my queen. Soon, you and I will be the new age Bonnie and Clyde. The world ain't seen nothing yet, Sugar." I smile and nod in agreement because yes, he ain't seen nothing yet.

CHAPTER 8

Corey

SITTING HERE LISTENING to what sounds like Baylor and Kye making out pisses me off. I have no right to feel like this, but I'm jealous. I'm infuriated and fucking jealous that the bastard gets to kiss her, and all I can do is sit here and listen. Ripping off my headphones, I throw them onto the table and stand up. Gripping the back of my neck, I stare down at the file before me and shake my head. There's shit everywhere right now.

My eyes land on a photo of Baylor and Creed Dawson. This Creed guy is Kye's go-to man. Picking up the photo, I stare at it, well, I stare at her. She's sitting in a car with him, and doesn't have a care in the world. I wish I could be as carefree as she is.

Dropping the photo, I continue to stare at her. Then I look to Creed and I decide to focus on him. Sifting through the mess, I find his file and begin to read. Seems that Baylor is connected to him through her sister's best friend, Cressida Bayliss. No one has spoken to Ms. Bayliss so I decide to take a little trip and visit her.

Grabbing my things, I head down to my car and drive over to her place. Pulling up, I turn the car off and climb out. I walk up the stairs and knock on the door. An attractive woman opens the door and stares at me through the screen. "Can I help you?" she cautiously asks.

"I hope so. I'm looking for Cressida Bayliss," I state.

"That's me. I'm Cress," she says, her face etched with hesitation.

"I'm Agent Corey Cox, I'd like to ask you a few questions about Creed Dawson."

"Is he okay?" she asks, her voice raising an octave.

"As far as I'm aware, yes. Can you tell me about your relationship with him?"

She opens the screen door and steps out onto the porch. "Creed and I dated for a few years about five years ago. He's the father of my daughter, Lexi." She pauses. "Is he in trouble?"

"I'm not at liberty to discuss that, but he is someone we are looking into."

"Fucking asshole," she whispers, "I knew something was up."

That statement piques my interest. "How so?" I ask.

"He's changed recently." Those three words concern me and I'm not liking where this conversation is heading. "He's become verbally abusive toward me. He's telling Lex horrible things about me and when she comes home, she's upset. Lately she hasn't been enjoying herself when she's with him."

"How old is your daughter?"

"She's five."

"When was the last time you saw Mr. Dawson?"

"Probably a week ago when he dropped Lexi off, but he's texted me a few times. Do I need to be worried about him with my daughter?"

"You know him better than I do, Ms. Bayliss, but trust your judgment. You seem like a smart woman." She nods at me, but I notice that all the color has drained from her face. "Can I ask what your relationship with him is now?"

"Civil, I guess." She shrugs.

"No, I mean, personally?"

"We aren't in a physical relationship, if that's what you mean. He's the father, if you can call him that, of my daughter and that's it. I spend as little time with him as possible."

"Why is that?"

"He's a dick," she honestly tells me. "If it wasn't for Lexi, he wouldn't be in my life at all. I tolerate him for Lexi and for her only."

I'm processing her words when a deep voice says, "Cress, is everything okay?"

She looks over my shoulder at the man and nods, then she looks back at me, "As I said, Agent Cox, apart from handover with my daughter, I don't know what Creed gets up to. Hell, I don't even know where he lives."

Well, this was a bust, I think to myself. "Okay, well thank you for your time, Ms. Bayliss." Pulling a card out, I hand it to her. "If you think of anything else, please don't hesitate to contact me."

Nodding at her and the guy, I turn around and head back to my car. Once I'm behind the wheel, I open the file and stare at the surveillance photo of Creed Dawson. This guy is a smarmy son of a bitch, he's a loose cannon, and I don't like the feeling that's developing in my stomach when it comes to him. He's almost as crazy as Kye, but whereas Kye is calm, cool, and collected, this guy is a crazy psychopath.

My phone's alarm goes off reminding me to head over to Baylor's for our first catch-up in an hour. When I think of her, I think about what I heard before I came here and I grind my teeth. Why does the fact she was making out with Vlahos irk me so much?

Putting my car into drive, I head back to the headquarters so I can change and pick up my 'work' van.

Forty-five minutes later, I pull up to Baylor and Avery's apartment. These overalls are uncomfortable as fuck. With everything I need in hand, I head into the building. Taking the stairs rather than the elevator, I step onto their floor and walk toward their apartment.

Raising my hand, I knock. I can sense her shuffling on the other side, and when the door swings open, I'm taken aback at the vision before me. Baylor is wearing a white halter dress that hugs her curves and highlights her tits perfectly. On her feet are purple heels that elongate her legs, and I imagine her legs wrapped about my waist. The heels digging into my ass as I kiss the life out of her. Her voice snaps my attention back to the present. "Are you going to come in? Or are you just going to stand there and eye-fuck me?"

"Watch your mouth, Kitten."

"Stop fucking calling me Kitten."

"Meow," I say, as I step around her and inside. As I walk past her, I'm assaulted with her scent. It's sweet, like candy, the total opposite of her personality, which is dark and musty. I walk over to the sofa and sit, pulling out my files and stare up at her.

"Make yourself at home, why don't you?" she sasses.

"Thanks, I will. So got anything for me?"

"Nope," she states, as she sits next to me.

"Maybe if you stop making out with him, you'd have something for me," I vehemently snap at her, my words shocking me. I'm being extremely unprofessional right now, but Baylor brings out this side of me. I stand, needing to get away from her right now; I walk around the coffee table and stare over at her.

"I've kissed him once and that was after he was shot and stitched up."

"So you kiss anyone if they've been shot?"

"I'd like to fucking shoot you," she sassily snaps at me.

"Feeling's mutual, Kitten."

She stands and storms over to me and pokes me in the chest. "Stop. Fucking. Calling. Me. Kitten."

"Stop making out with the suspect and do your job."

We stand toe to toe, staring at one another. Something passes between us. The air thickens, much like my dick. Reaching over, I grip her cheeks in my palms and slam my lips to hers. She covers my hands and deepens the kiss. My tongue slides in and out of her mouth, while she wraps her leg around me, pulling us closer. Our kiss is frenzied and carnal. The sound of keys sliding into the front door lock grabs my attention. I push Baylor away from me, just as the front door opens and Avery walks in.

"Sorry, I'm late," she says. "Traffic was terrible." She looks over to us. Both of us are disheveled and breathing heavily. "What's going on?"

I'm at a loss for words right now; I have never acted so unprofessionally in all of my career. This woman causes my brain to stop functioning.

"I was telling Agent Cox here how I kissed Kye this morning, getting him to trust me the only way I know possible."

"Whoring yourself?" I say, and as soon as I say those two words, I instantly regret them.

"I'm just doing as you told me," she says, turning to face me. "You told me to do whatever it takes to bring Kye to his knees and trust me, I did exactly that." She winks and turns her attention back to Ave. "How was your day, sis?"

Her nonchalant actions piss me off but at the same time, I'm more turned on than I ever have been before. This woman is going to be the death of me...and possibly my career.

CHAPTER 9
Baylor

HOLY FUCK, Cox is kissing me, and holy fuck, can this man kiss. Corey-fucking-Cox sure knows how to kiss a woman. I'm ready to rip my dress over my head, turn around, and let him fuck me senseless over the arm of the sofa, but Ave arrives and prevents that from happening. Thankfully...I think. When he calls me a whore, I see red and any feelings of wanting to fuck disappear as quickly as they came.

The next words out of my mouth are complete bullshit but fuck him. "...You told me to do whatever it takes to bring Kye to his knees and trust me, I did exactly that." I throw him a wink and poke my tongue into my cheek, insinuating I gave Kye a blow job.

Turning to face Ave, I smile sweetly. "How was your day, sis?"

"Good," she drawls the word out. She can sense she's walked in on something but she's too nice to state the obvious.

"That's great," I tell her, she stares at me. Imploring with her eyes for me to say something, but I'm at a loss to explain it right now. One minute we're bickering and the next, he's tongue fucking me. And can I say, it was the best tongue fucking of my life...I can only imagine what he'd be like between the sheets.

Shaking my head, those dirty disappear and I come back to the present to hear Ave and Cox talking about Creed. "...he's a dick. Plain and simple."

"That's putting it lightly," I add, "He's a crazy mother-fucking dickwad." He eyes me intently. My body and clit is aware of his intense stare. It's getting annoying so, being the mature woman I am, I stick my tongue out at him and smirk.

"As I was saying, he's psycho crazy." I look over to Ave, "What did Cressida ever see in him?"

She shrugs. "Beats me. If it wasn't for Lexi, she wouldn't have anything to do with Dickwad Dawson."

"That's the best nickname for him. Lexi is a cute kid. She's sassy like her mom." Ave looks at me in confusion. "Dickwad stopped by with her the other day."

Her eyes widen. "Don't worry, Kye put a stop to that. He lost his shit when he saw her there with him."

"Who brings their kid to a place like that?" Cox asks.

In unison, Ave and I both say, "A dickwad." Then we laugh. In the last few weeks, our twin thing is returning.

"I'll give it to Kye," I add, "he refuses to hurt woman and children."

"Tell that to his sister and mother," Cox says.

My eyes snap to his. "They were killed by accident. He didn't want to hurt them." My defense of Kye is confusing right now.

"Accident or not, Kye's actions killed his mother and sister. Don't underestimate this man, Ms. Evans. Given the chance, he will end you too. I've seen men like him change in the blink of an eye. As they garner more power, it goes to their head and clouds their judgement. Kye Vlahos is a classic sociopath, please bear that in mind." The room falls silent and we process his words. "And with that, we'll wrap up today's meet. I'll see you again in three days' time. Unless you uncover something before then."

"Thank you, Agent Cox," Ave says, ever the polite one. "So far, you are holding up your end and keeping Bay safe."

"Please, I'm keeping myself safe. See you soon, Cox," I say, waving at him with a sweet smile on my face.

With that, he turns and walks toward the door. Ave says goodbye and closes the door behind him. She turns to face me, and I smile at her, "Thank you," I say.

"What for?"

"For always having my back. For always being by my side."

She walks over to me, throws her arm around my shoulder, and pulls me in for a side hug. "I'll stand by you, Bay. Always. I won't let anybody hurt you. You're my twinsie." She grabs my hand and leads me into the kitchen.

"And I won't let anyone hurt you either," I tell her, and I mean it. After what Smallie and River did to her, thinking she was me; I knew I had to make up for it, and my past actions too. "And I'll stop hurting you too. You're my twinsie, Avie, and I'm sorry. So so sorry for all that I've done and how I've treated you recently. You've always been on Team Baylor and I've let you down, but this is my chance to make you proud."

"And I am, Bay. I'm so proud of you right now for owning your mistakes, I just wish it was in a safe 'non-bring-down-a-mafia-drug-ring' way."

We stare at one another and a calmness washes over me. I know Avie and I will be fine. We will get back to our BayBay and Avie selves and be happier than we've ever been.

"Hey, Bay," she says, breaking the silence.

"Yeah, what's up, Avie?"

"Are you subconsciously singing that *I'll stand by you* song right now?"

"Yes." We both laugh. She grabs her phone, pulls up Spotify and clicks play. I open a bottle of red and pour us two glasses of wine. With our drinks in hand, we head into the living room and sit on the sofa. We listen as Chrissie Hynde from the Pretenders sings "I'll Stand By You." We join in singing the chorus, but Ave and I aren't half as good as Chrissie.

The song finishes and as is the emotional roller coaster that is Spotify random, we are now listening to "Butterfly" by Crazy Town.

Ave turns the volume down and looks over at me. I can tell from the look in the eye, she's about to interrogate me regarding what she walked in on. I was secretly hoping she'd forget, but Ave doesn't forget anything. "Okay, so…" She drags out the word so, waiting for me to talk.

"So what?" I ask, playing coy, but I know exactly what Ave's referring to…the kiss. The fucking out-of-this-world kiss that rocked me to my core.

"What did I walk in on earlier?" She raises her hand to silence me when I go to deny it. She gives me the 'don't mess with me' teacher look. "I have eyes, Bay, and I could feel the tension between you and Corey."

Not sure how to answer, I pick up my wine glass and chug back the contents. Since my glass is now empty, I stand up and walk back into the kitchen. Topping up my glass, I grab a new bottle and the open one, and walk back into the living room.

"Wow, a second bottle, this must be good," Ave teases.

"Not sure I'd describe it as good."

"Well, how would you describe it then?"

"Confusing in an already precarious situation."

"Okay, well start at the beginning and tell me."

"Cox and I kissed just before you arrived. One minute we were arguing about me kissing Kye and the next, he was tongue fucking me. If you hadn't walked in, I would have begged for him to bend me over the sofa and fuck me."

"You kissed Kye?" she questions.

"That's what you're focusing on now?"

"Well, yeah, I'll get to the Cox kissing but first, why did you kiss Kye? And how does Cox know?"

"There's a listening thingy-ma-giggy in my phone. Kye got stabbed—"

"What? How?"

"With a knife," I cheekily say, as Ave eyes me. "He was out with Creed and returned stabbed. Monica, his bimbo bitch doctor came and stitched him up, they've fucked before and I saw red. Don't know why I got angry, but I did. He found me and then we kissed, but while I was kissing him, I was picturing Cox. I stopped it before it went further. Anyway, Cox brought it up before you arrived, and then he kissed me and I kissed him back. Then you came home, and well, you know the rest."

"That's a lot of kissing," she says.

"Yep," I say letting the P pop. "And it will never happen again...with either of them."

"Bay, I don't believe you."

I look at her, purse my lips, and shake my head. "Yeah, I don't believe myself either."

We both fall silent and sip on our wine then Ave breaks the silence. "Can I ask you a question?" I nod my head, "Who's the better kisser?"

Without thinking, I blurt out, "Cox."

"That doesn't surprise me. That man is fine. I wonder what he's packing."

"Avery Evans," I playfully scold, "what has gotten into you?"

"Flynn," she replies with a wink. I shake my head.

"You dirty, dirty girl. What has happened to my sweet and innocent sister?"

"She met a sexy-as-sin Irish doctor, who makes her do things she would never ever do."

"Like what?" I ask. Ave and I really haven't had a chance to chat about her new relationship.

"Well, the night we met, not only did I have my first one-night stand but I also let him finger fuck me in the restroom alcove at The Tavern."

"Is it wrong that I'm kind of proud of you regarding this?"

"Cress said something similar." She takes a sip then adds, "I think Corey might be your Flynn."

"Nah, I need this to be over so I can forget about Corey-fucking-Cox."

"You really think you can forget about him after this?"

"I have to. We are too different. It would never work between us."

"Flynn and I are total opposites," she says. "We work." I ponder her words and wonder, could Cox and I be more than whatever the hell we are right now?

"You two are a classic opposites attract, I'm glad that my stupidity didn't ruin that for you because I have never seen you happier."

"Flynn makes me happy, he brings me out of my shell. I miss not seeing him when he's on nights." I realize that I too become sad when I don't see Cox. He has wormed his way into my cold, dead heart, but we can be nothing more than informant and handler. Maybe if we'd met under other circumstances, I could see us working out, but I'm a criminal and he's the law. He hates me and I, I don't know how I feel about him.

For the rest of the evening, Ave and I listen to music, drink wine, and hang out, just like we used to. It's the perfect way to end a stressful and confusing day.

Later that night, as I lie in bed, I think over everything that has happened and how my life has changed. Things concerning Agent Corey Cox are blurring and I don't know what to do. And that scares the living shit out of me.

CHAPTER 10
Corey

IT'S BEEN two weeks since I kissed Baylor and ever since then it's all I've thought about. Hell, I've even jerked off in the shower with visions of her on her knees. Her pouty lips wrapped around my shaft as it slides in and out of her mouth. Fuck, my dick is hard once again.

Thankfully I'm alone right now. I readjust myself and look across the road, still no movement. I'm staking out the doctor who has been working with the Vlahos family for the last few years. Flipping open the file, I reread the details regarding Dr. Monica Quinn. She's thirty-four years old. Graduated top of her class from Johns Hopkins and now runs a practice in the burbs. How does a successfully doctor like her end up working for the mafia? The door opens and out walks the lady of the hour. When I see her in person, I can see why she's their doctor. She has dark brown hair, killer legs, and massive fake tits. Why women do that to themselves amazes me.

She climbs into her black Mercedes and pulls out of the practice parking lot. Starting my car, I follow her keeping my distance and changing lanes to make sure she doesn't know I'm following her. She pulls up to a restaurant and stops at the valet. She flirts with the pimply faced teenager and walks into the restaurant. A few moments later, Kye and Creed arrive.

Her face lights up when she sees Kye and what shocks me most is the kiss that occurs between Monica and Kye. I thought he only had eyes for Baylor. This development doesn't sit well with me. I make a note to discuss it with her later. And speak of the devil, her ride drops her off at the front doors and she walks into the restaurant. Her head held high, showing just how strong she is.

From my spot on the street, I see that Baylor is unimpressed as she joins them. Grabbing my laptop off the passenger seat, I log into the surveillance system and hope that I can hear what's going on. Baylor must have her phone on the table because I can hear everything clearly.

"Baylor, Sugar. Calm down," Kye says.

"Do not fucking tell me to calm down. This bitch had her hands all over you."

"That's not all I had on him," Monica says to Baylor, taunting her. Oh, how I wish I was inside to witness this scene unfold live. Right now, I'm imagining Baylor's face turning purple, her fists will be clenched, and she'll be biting her bottom lip in frustration.

"You are fucking dead," Baylor seethes, "Either she goes, or I go."

"There's the door," Monica throws at Baylor.

"Enough," Kye growls. "Ladies, play nice. Baylor, we need Monica."

"There are a million doctors in the world, I say we get another," Baylor huffs.

"I quite like this one," Creed adds, the tone of his voice chilling.

"Of course, you would," Baylor snarks, "you like all the hoity-toity bitches."

"What can I say, I have a type."

"Thank fuck, I'm not your type," Baylor says, and right now I'm imagining her crossing her arms defiantly.

"Well, now that's out of the way. We have business to discuss."

"I need a drink, if she's going to be here," Baylor snarls.

"Day drinking, really?" Monica says. "Why is she even here, Kye? Why do you need her?"

"She's my queen. She'll be by my side always. You can be replaced, Monica; Baylor cannot. There is only one queen and Baylor is it."

"You say such nice things," Baylor answers. "So what's the plan, Stan?"

"Don't ever call me that again," Kye snaps, reminding me of when Baylor said that to me. "The plan is in motion, specifics are still being nutted out, but I need to know that the three of you are all on board?"

All three of them nod and say yes.

"Excellent." Kye explains, "The world won't know what hit it when this all comes to fruition."

"Wanna fill us in on the specifics?" Baylor asks.

"All in due time, my queen. All in due time."

They fall into general chitchat. I need to see Baylor so I take the opportunity. I exit my car and cross the street and head inside. Baylor sees me and her eyes widen, I nod toward the restroom as I take my seat at a table nearby, placing my back to them.

A few moments later, she walks by toward the restrooms. I order a drink from the waiter and after he leaves, I stand and follow Baylor. She's waiting in the alcove just near the restrooms.

"What the fuck are you doing here?" she snarls at me.

"Getting lunch," I nonchalantly say, "and—"

"I know, I know," she sasses, "language."

"Having fun antagonizing the good doctor?" She growls at me. "Are you jealous of her?"

"Pffft, please. There's no comparison between her and me." *I agree,* I silently think as my gaze roams over her. She's wearing a deep purple dress and what I have come to realize, her favorite purple strappy heels. "Now, what do you want?"

"Yes," a deep voice says from behind us. "What do you want with my queen?"

Turning around, I come face-to-face with Kye Vlahos. "I'm her contractor, Corey." I stretch out my hand. Kye looks down at it, then to Baylor and finally, he shakes. Squeezing harder than necessary to exert his power. I don't cower. I look him directly in the eye and do not waver. "I'm here meeting a potential new client and when I saw Ms. Evans, I thought I'd give her an update on the tiles. They were damaged in transit and there's now going to be a delay. We will need to extend the completion date by a few weeks."

"Ave will be upset," Baylor replies, "but these things take time. I'm sure it will all work out in the end." I get the double meaning to her words and nod.

"All the planning and waiting will be worth it in the end. You just need to keep your eye on the prize."

"I've already got my prize," Kye says, pulling Baylor into his side and kissing her temple. She smiles up at him but it doesn't reach her eyes. I start to wonder if maybe this is too much for her. Did I make a mistake sending her in?

I realize they are both staring at me. "Well, I must run," I tell them. "I'll be in touch, Ms. Evans, when I know more."

"Mmmhmpf," she nonchalantly replies. "See ya."

She takes Kye's hand and pulls him away. They walk back over to their table, say their goodbyes, and I watch them leave. They really are a stunning couple and she's playing the doting queen role well, but a feeling of unease is building. My gut has never let me down before, I hope this isn't the first time it does.

CHAPTER 11

Baylor

THE FOLLOWING DAY, I'm lazing at home with a slight hangover. Okay, a massive hangover. After running into Cox with Kye, I was antsy and not feeling myself. After the meeting, I returned to the apartment and was happy to see Ave was home. Just like we did the other week, we spent the evening together. We shared two bottles of red wine, watched *Ten Things I Hate About You*—hello Heath Ledger—and threw together an antipasto platter for dinner. I think I was Greek in a past life because I could live off wine, cheese, olives, and cured meats.

The serenity of my morning is broken when I get a frantic call from Kye. He needs me to meet him at a restaurant downtown immediately. He tells me to dress provocatively in a skimpy slutty dress. *Fuck him*, I think to myself as I walk into my room and grab out a pair of skintight leather pants, a black halter top with a deep V and, you guessed it, my purple strappy heels. "Perfect," I whisper to my reflection, before I add some nude lipstick and blow wave my blonde locks.

Not skanky-sexy like he requested, but I'm still fucking hot and that's all that matters.

Grabbing my clutch, I throw in my lip gloss, gum, some cash, and I'm ready to go. On my way out the door, I order an Uber. I'm waiting on the curb when Kye calls. I answer on the second ring, "Hey!"

"Where the fuck are you? When I tell you to come, you come."

"Calm your tits, asshole. I'm waiting for an Uber."

"Why are you Ubering?"

"I don't have a car," I tell him. "I always Uber it."

"Well, fucking get one," he snaps, seems this will be a fun afternoon. "No queen of mine Ubers it."

"Sure, I'll just whip thirty-seven grand outta my ass and go buy myself a Mini Cooper convertible." We both go silent just as my Uber pulls up. "My ride's here, see you soon." I hang up and mumble, "Fuck you," to my phone as I climb into the car.

Staring out the window, I sigh. Cox was right, Kye is a sociopath, but I'll raise the bar and add controlling dick-faced asshole. His actions are becoming unhinged, and to be honest, he scares the absolute crap out of me. He's definitely not the man I knew and loved, but I don't have a choice. I need to do this if I want to redeem myself, but at times like today, I question if it's all worth in the end.

The car pulls up at the restaurant and I thank the driver. I look up and see Kye staring at me from inside the restaurant. I smile but he doesn't smile back and a sinking feeling develops in the pit of my stomach. Putting one foot in front of the other, I head inside. I repeat to myself over and over. "I'm tough, I'll get through this." And I hope to high heaven that I do get through this.

To say the afternoon with Kye was fun would be a lie. It was a shitshow from the moment I stepped into the restaurant, but I showed him that no one fucks with me. I think I finally proved to him that I'm with him one-hundred-percent, no thanks to Cox anyway.

Walking over to see Kye, I see Creed and two other men sitting at the table. "Gentlemen," I say, as I take the empty seat next to Kye. His eyes roam over me and I see anger reflecting back at me.

"I said wear a dress," he barks at me.

"No one tells me what to wear," I tell him.

Reaching over to grab his drink, he grabs my wrist and squeezes. "Are you defying me?" he growls, increasing pressure around my wrist.

"This isn't nineteen twenty, asshole. I will dress however the fuck I want. If you don't like it, I'm quite happy to leave."

The grip Kye has on my wrist tightens, it's becoming painful but I refuse to show him that. Thankfully, one of the men sitting across from us breaks our Mexican stand-off. "She's a live one."

Turning my gaze from Kye to the man, I raise my eyebrows at him in a 'what the fuck' way and at the same time, I pull my wrist free from Kye.

"And you are?" I ask, just as the waitress places a lychee martini in front of me. Looking to Kye, I smile my thanks and pick me drink. I take a sip and the liquor instantly calms me.

Licking my lips, I smile at the men as Kye introduces us. "Bay, my queen, this is Max and Bob." Those names ring a bell, but they also cause me to laugh because they are dog names. "We are discussing a new business partnership. I was hoping you can help sway their decision to join forces with us."

Placing my drink on the table, I turn to face Kye. "Are you whoring me out to Max and Bob?" My voice is cool and calm, but on the inside, Bitchy Baylor is raging. I'm no whore and he needs to remember that. He shrugs at me and that pisses me off.

Leaning into him, I breathe heavily on his neck as I slide my hand up his thigh. Palming his cock through his slacks, I increase the pressure. Licking up his neck, I whisper, "I'm no one's whore." I bite his earlobe and squeeze his dick hard in my fist. He clenches his teeth and hisses from the pain. "If you want me to be your queen, you need to remember that."

Letting go of his cock, I turn my attention to the men across from us. "Now, gentlemen," I purr, picking up my drink and staring across the table, "let's see if we can come to some other agreement that doesn't involve me and my virtue." Taking another sip, I watch the men.

"I like her," Max says to Kye, throwing a wink at me before he looks at Bob. The two of them have a silent conversation oblivious to myself, Kye, and Creed sitting here. I've nearly finished my drink when they turn their attention back to us. "You have yourself a deal, Vlahos," Bob confirms.

While Max adds, "On one condition." His eyes are locked on me as he says this and surprisingly, I don't cower under his gaze.

"Anything," Kye replies whereas I say, "Depends."

Both men laugh. "We want her," he points to me, "on the first drop. No Queen B., no deal."

"As long as it doesn't interrupt my schedule, or involve me on my back, I'm sure I can oblige." I have no clue what I'm agreeing to but this could give me the intel that Cox needs, and it will also reaffirm to Kye that I'm on his side. He's still keeping me at an arm's length. I need to do something that doesn't involve me sleeping with him. I won't go there again, my legs are closed to Kye Vlahos. Even if he wasn't a scary mafia king, that boat has sailed.

"Now, hold up a minute," Kye interjects, slamming his fist on the table, the cutlery rattling from the force. "I'm the boss here. I have the final say in things."

Turning my gaze to him, I sweetly smile. "And here I thought we were in this together, babe."

"Uh-oh, trouble in paradise," Creed teases.

Kye growls and turns his attention back to me. "You may be my queen but I am the motherfucking king. I have the final say."

"Whatever," I nonchalantly reply. Leaning back in my chair, I cross my arms, unintentionally pushing up my breasts. Four sets of eyes drop to my chest. *Men,* I think to myself as I lean forward, showing off the girls even more. If I lean forward any more, my nipples will be showing. I'm not prepared to whore myself but I will be a dick tease.

After a few more seconds, I reach out, pick up my martini, lean back, and sip. *The titty show is over, boys.* The four of them watch my movements intently. Looking at Kye, I see anger and lust reflecting back at me. Max and Bob are still staring at my tits; I see hunger in their eyes but also fear. They don't want to cross Kye, but at the same time, they are men, thinking with their dicks when the hint of boob is placed before them. When I look over to Creed, I shudder. His eyes are glued to my chest and the creepy fucker is licking his lips. Whereas Bob and Max's glare is playful, Creed's is deranged and dirty—I really hate that fucker.

Biting my lip, I hold back my smirk when Kye smiles. Finally, I am the fucking queen Kye wants me to be and I have four hapless pawns trapped in the valley of my breasts.

The word pawn takes me back to a conversation with Cox and for the first time, I think that he's right. I can do this, I can bring down Kye, and I will do whatever it takes to do so.

The next few weeks are much of the same: lunches with associates, new and old. Kye parading me around like a shiny new toy, showing off his queen to his minions.

In public, we are the ultimate power couple but behind closed doors, we live separate lives. There has been no further kissing Kye, or Cox, and I'm pretty sure he's still fucking that doctor bitch, but I don't care. At the end of the day, I'm his queen and that's all I need to be to get this done.

Besides, I'm lusting after the one person I should not be lusting over, Corey Cox.

Each night, as I drift off to sleep, I have inappropriate steamy dreams starring my sexy but annoying agent. I wake up and pleasure myself, whispering his name as my fingers bring me to climax. My digits are getting a good work out at the moment; maybe I'll need to invest in a B.O.B to give them a rest. Nah, it's the real deal or nothing for me.

After our meeting this week, Cox seems impressed with the intel I'm gathering, but it's still not enough to bring everything crumbling down around Kye. I've fully gained his trust now, but some days I feel like one of his lap dogs. Being at his beck and call. Dropping everything when he calls and running straight to him, well, driving to him in my new navy blue Mini Cooper convertible. A perk of being his queen, as well as a stylish new wardrobe.

After the Max and Bob wardrobe argument, he sent me on a shopping spree with a predetermined list of clothes. Thankfully, he wasn't with me so I could get the requested items but in the style I like. I've never had such an amazing wardrobe before, totally makes up for Creed being around.

As Cox promised, I'm safe and we have been able to keep up the ruse of him being my and Ave's contractor. Not sure how much longer we can use that cover but fingers crossed, I won't have to do this much longer because Kye is starting to scare me with his behavior. Cox was right, the power and control is going to his head. I need to end this and I need to end it soon. The sooner, the better,

CHAPTER 12

Corey

IT'S BEEN ALMOST three months and I'm no closer to bringing down Kye Vlahos. The list of associate names I'm gathering from Baylor is great, but I need that smoking gun. I need that one piece of evidence that will close this close, bring it to an end, and put Kye behind bars for a very long time. The only downfall to that is my time with my Kitten will come to an end. As much as she is a pain in the ass, she's also intriguing and has piqued my interest.

We'd never work out as a couple. She's wild. I'm not. She's a criminal. I'm a law enforcement officer. We are two opposites, and there's the little fact she hates me. There's a fine line between love and hate, and we are teetering precariously on that line.

Throwing the file onto my desk, I rub the back of my neck in frustration. I'm starting to lose hope that this is going to work. I begin to wonder if sending Baylor in was the right thing to do when I'm given the Hail-fucking-Mary of all Hail Marys.

A knock on the door grabs my attention and I look up to see Oats standing there with a goofy grin on his face. "Hey, what's up?"

"Creed Dawson was arrested for assault."

"Come again?" I say, totally shocked at what I just heard.

"He attacked his ex-partner, Cressida Bayliss, earlier this evening."

"Shit, is she okay?"

"She's extremely lucky. Her mom happened to be driving past when he attacked. Mom called the current boyfriend and he managed to get there in time. Dawson was about to rape her."

"Fucking hell. I knew he was a psychopath, but that's just nuts."

"Thought you might want to talk to him, see if you can get anything from him regarding Vlahos and his plans."

"Yeah, thanks. I'll be right there."

Leaning back in my chair, I grin. Creed Dawson's arrest could work in my favor. If he's as delusional as Baylor says he is, I'm willing to bet my left nut he will sing like a fucking canary to reduce his time.

With a pep in my step, I walk into the interrogation room, his eyes widen when he sees me. "You," he snarls, "you're Baylor's contractor."

"One of my many jobs," I tell him, as I take a seat across from him. "So, Creed, I have a proposition for you."

"Thanks for the offer, asshole, but I don't suck cock."

"My cock isn't on the table but your ass can be. I'm sure Tiny in cell block 'C' would just love you and your ass."

His eyes widen. "What the fuck, man? What have I ever done to you?"

"Me? Nothing, but you attacked the mother of your child and you were about to rape her. Tiny doesn't much care for assholes who beat on women."

"Bitch fucking deserved it," he snarls, glaring at me.

"And you will deserve everything Tiny will give you, but..." I leave it hanging, waiting to see what he will do.

"But what?" he asks, all malice in his voice gone and I know I have him.

"You help me and I'll help you."

"How can I help you? I'm no one."

"You're not no one to Kye Vlahos."

His eyes widen at the mention of Kye. "What the fuck does he have to do with this?"

"I've been building a case against him, I need your help to wrap it up nice and neatly, so I can get my person safely out of there."

"You don't have an agent in there. Kye would sniff a fed out in a heartbeat."

"Never said it was a fed."

"Who, then?"

"I can't play all my cards in the first hand, can I? Now, Mr. Dawson, are you going to help me? Or should I give Tiny a call?"

"What do you want to know?"

BINGO! This is too fucking easy. I knew he'd turn. I didn't expect him to roll over so easily. I don't trust this asshole, so I'll be cautious with what he does tell me. Deciding to push my luck, I lean forward. "Everything. I want to know every single thing about Kye Vlahos and his organization."

"And you'll keep me out of jail? Away from Tiny? Safe from him?"

"Depending on the intel you give me, I'll do what I can."

"All right then. Kye Vlahos is a crazy motherfucker. You name it, he's into it."

"Be more specific or I'll tell Tiny you like it rough. The rougher, the better."

"Guns. Drugs. Human trafficking."

"Elaborate on the human trafficking."

"He needs men for labor."

"So no women and children?"

"Not women and children. He has a conscience."

A laugh escapes me, the fact he won't traffic women and children doesn't mean shit. Trafficking is trafficking and with all of this, he's going down for a very long time. "So when he hears that you beat the mother of his child, he'll let you go scot-free?" Creed's face pales as he registers what I just said. "I need specifics if you want my help and protection."

"Kye and that bitch." The mention of Baylor piques my interest. It feels like she's hiding her involvement in all of this and Creed here will either confirm my suspicion or prove me wrong. I don't have any proof she's deceiving me, but the doubt is there. But then again, Kye is keeping her at a distance because I don't think he trusts her either. *Which team are you on Baylor: Team Kye? Or Team Cox?*

"Which bitch are we referring to?"

"Baylor Evans. She's a smart one. Always there, plotting and planning. I don't trust her."

"And why's that?"

"That whore took my place as his number one. She opened her legs and he fell for it."

"So you're jealous because Kye is getting some from her?"

"I'm not jealous, I'm pissed off. She waltzes in after two of my men are mysteriously killed while retrieving her. I call bullshit. A little slut like her couldn't take down two men like that." His eyes widen when realization hits. "She's your insider. You were the ones to kill Smallie and River."

Shaking my head, I deny everything. "I'm not telling you who I have on the inside. And I'm not discussing some woman you're jealous of. I want Vlahos, I don't care about his bitch."

"It's her, it has to be. No one else would be stupid enough to cross him. That fucking whore is a dead bitch when Kye finds out."

"And you'll be a dead man if Kye finds out you ratted." His eyes widen once again. "I can't protect you, Mr. Dawson, unless you give me something to pin on him. So far, everything you've told me is in line with what I already know. I need something concrete from you for me to hold up the end of my bargain."

"There's a meet later this week, Kye is getting all the big players in to take them out. He wants more control. He wants to own the world."

"Now, that wasn't so hard, was it?" I tell him, sliding a notepad and pencil across to him. "I want names, a date, and a location for this meet."

Picking up the pencil, he starts writing. I'm not sure I trust this guy, I need to meet with Baylor and confirm everything Creed tells me, but can I trust what she's saying? If Dawson knew about this meet, why didn't she tell me? Or is this Kye keeping her in the dark again? I need to meet with her and see if she's withholding information from me and confirm, once and for all, what side she's on.

With the info from Creed in hand, I exit the room and call Baylor. Calling is risky but time is of the essence. "Hello?" a deep male voice I recognize as Kye Vlahos answers after the second ring.

"I'm looking for Baylor."

"And you are?"

"Her contractor. And you are?"

"Her king." Hearing him call himself that really pisses me off and makes the urge to take him down even stronger.

"Is she there? I need to speak with her urgently."

"She's tied up right now," I don't like his tone of voice, but before he can say anything, I hear her yelling in the background. "What the fuck are you doing with my phone?"

Their voices are muffled, but I can hear her yell, 'Fuck you, asshole!" A door slams, and I finally hear her through the line, "Hey, this is Baylor."

"It's Cox," I sternly say, my tone harsher than I intended.

"What can I do for you?" she sweetly says, and just hearing her voice calms the rage building within me.

"We need to meet as soon as possible."

"Sure, I can meet you at the apartment. Is there another issue with the project?"

Her comment stumps me and then I remember I'm her 'contractor.' "Kinda."

"Okay, well, I'll see you in an hour or so."

"Great, see you then." I hang up and smile. She really is in this for the right reasons. Creed is just getting in my head and trying to throw me off my game. With the end in sight, I need to focus on my endgame: bringing Kye Vlahos to justice. Grabbing my things, I head to my car and make my way to Baylor's place.

I'm parked out front but I don't see Baylor's car so I sit, wait, and watch. When Baylor finally arrives, I watch as she exits her new car and heads inside. I wait a few moments and then climb out of my work truck and head to her apartment.

She answers the door straightaway after I knock. "Hey," she says, but the smile she gives me doesn't reach her eyes. She looks tired and uneasy.

"You okay?" I ask as I step inside.

"Fine," she drawls, but from the tone of her voice, she is anything but fine.

"Kitten," I plead.

"I'm in a mood 'cause Kye's in a mood 'cause Creed was arrested and—"

"I know Creed was," I say, my confession shocking her.

"How do you know?"

"I know everything regarding Kye Vlahos and his crew. Seems you've been holding out on me."

"I've told you everything I know," she snaps at me, flopping down on the sofa and crossing her arms like a petulant child.

"Really? Everything?"

"Yes," she says, but her eyes dart around the apartment anxiously. The fact she won't look at me confirms she's hiding something.

"Look at me," I say and she lifts her gaze to me. "Thursday. 2:00 p.m."

"Is that supposed to mean something?"

"You tell me."

"What fucking game are you playing, Cox?"

We stare at one another. "Kitten, a source of mine tells me an important meeting is happening on Thursday with quite a few big players."

She scoffs and shrugs her shoulders. "This is news to me." From the look on her face, I believe her.

"I believe you," I confirm. "We're going to make our move on Thursday. I don't want you at that meeting."

"What do I do if Kye wants me there?"

"Lie. Cheat. Whatever. Just do not be at that meeting, Baylor. Please?"

"Okay," she says. She bites her bottom lip. "This is it, isn't it?"

I nod. "I think so."

She stands up and walks over to me. We stare at one another, "Cox, I, ummm—"

Her phone rings, breaking the spell that enveloped the two of us just now. She pulls out her phone. "Shit," she mumbles. "It's Kye."

"Answer it."

"Hey," she casually says. She listens to Kye and nods her head, saying, "Mmmhmpf," quite a few times. "Sure, I'll be there as soon as I finish with the contractor," she tells him. "Okay, see you soon." She hangs up and looks to me. "I, umm, ahh, have to go. Kye needs to see me."

"Okay, but remember what I said. Stay away from that meeting on Thursday."

We say our goodbyes and I walk out, leaving her alone in her apartment. This is what we've been working toward, but now that the end is in sight, I'm not ready for it to be over. I'm not ready to say goodbye to Baylor Evans, and that scares me.

CHAPTER 13

Baylor

ON THE DRIVE back to the warehouse, I play the meeting just now with Cox over and over in my mind. He's worried about me and it's not in the handler/informant way, it was in a caring I-don't-want-you-to-get-hurt kind of way. Before Kye called, I thought we might kiss again. I hoped to kiss him again and I think he wanted to kiss me too. I wanted to feel his lips pressed against mine. To have them all over my body. I wanted to strip him out of his suit and then lick him from head to toe, paying special attention to the appendage between his thighs.

I want him...but I can't have him. We are from two different worlds. Hell, we'd probably kill one another if we were under the same roof for longer than an hour.

As I pull up at the warehouse, it hits me; I'm falling for Agent Cox.

Shaking my head, I laugh, of course I fall for the one person I can never have; such is my life. Nothing can become of it because I'm me and he's him. I need to finish this job and then forget I ever met the sexy-as-fuck agent.

Sitting in my car, I stare at the steering wheel, feeling sad. I know I need to go inside but I can't. I want to drive away from here and never see Kye Vlahos ever again. A knock on the window startles me and I jump in fright. Looking up, I see Monica-fucking-Quinn staring at me. Seeing her here pisses me off. Any sadness I felt evaporates and is replaced with anger and brings Bitchy Baylor to the surface.

Pushing my door open, I step out. "What are you doing here?" My voice full of disdain, gives away how I feel about her being here.

"Kye called."

"So you come running whenever he calls you? Pathetic much?"

"Whatever," she sasses. "When he tires of you, he'll come back to me."

"Keep telling yourself that. I'm his queen; you are nothing but an employee of his. He only calls you when he needs you. I'm always here."

"I'm more than that," she mumbles quietly, but I hear it. Hearing those words piss me off and Bitchy Baylor makes an appearance.

"Say that to my face."

She steps to me, our noses millimeters apart. "I'm more than that. You might be his queen, but I'm the one he fucks."

"You're his fucking whore. Nothing more. Nothing less."

"You—" she snarls but Kye steps outside and interrupts, "Ladies, are you fighting over me?"

Arrogant dick, I think to myself, as I smile and look over to him. "You wish, dear," I tell him. "I was just telling the lovely doctor here that's she's nothing but your whore. You can fuck who you want as long as I stay your queen."

"And that is what you are, my queen." He cups my cheek and smiles at me. I shudder at his touch but thankfully there's a chill in the air. I can play it off as I'm cold, running my hands up and down my arms, trying to warm myself up. Leaning over, I place a kiss on his cheek. My gaze is locked on Monica. She's fuming right now. I think she thought she was more to him, but my words and his actions prove my point. The look on her face is priceless as realization sets in that she's nothing more than the mafia doctor and his side piece, a warm place to shove his cock.

Pulling back from Kye, I blow her a kiss and walk away, swinging my hips from side to side with each step away from them. Opening the door, I enter the warehouse. The only sound is my heels echoing off the cement floors, and with each step I take, my shitty mood evaporates. Nothing beats a good bitch smackdown and I just took Monica down without lifting a finger.

Pouring myself a glass of white wine, I fall into what's become my seat and wait for Kye and the doctor bitch to join us. As I sip on my wine, I smile to myself. The old Baylor would have been pissed that he was cheating on me, but the new me? Well she' doesn't give a flying fuck because she has the title of Queen and doesn't have to fuck Kye.

Kye finally joins me and I notice he's alone. The look in his eye right now is predatory and alarming. He pours himself a scotch and takes a seat next to me. He stares at me as he takes a drink, swirling the liquid around in his glass. "So… I called you here because I need you."

"What's new?" I cheekily say, lifting my glass to my lips. I drink and watch him over the rim.

He smirks at my snark. "I have a meeting set for Thursday afternoon. I want you there by my side. Showing everyone that we are the King and Queen of Chicago."

"I'm busy," I tell him, looking at my nails as if I'm bored, but in reality, I'm shitting bricks right now. This is what Cox warned me to stay away from not one hour ago. I need to get out of this but if I refuse, he'll know something is up. I'm so screwed and not in the fun, sweaty, naked way.

"Yeah, you're busy…with me." His tone is harsh and unnerving. "I need my queen with me at this meet, and if you want to keep being my queen, you'll be there."

The look in his eyes is scary. I've never seen him like this before. "Fine," I relent. "I'll be there." *Shit. Shit. Shit.*

"Like you had a choice." He places his hand on my thigh and squeezes tightly. I can feel his sinister gaze on me. "Are you hiding something from me, Sugar?"

Swallowing the sip I just took, I turn my head and stare into his eyes and smile sweetly. Leaning into him, I whisper, "Wouldn't you like to know?" Placing my glass on the coffee table, I stand and shuffle past him to head toward the bathroom.

My heart is pounding so loud that I don't hear Kye sneak up behind me. He roughly grabs the back of my shoulder and spins me to face him. His face is red with anger, "You may be my queen, but I am the fucking king. I can take you out whenever I want." He pulls me closer to him, one hand on my hip and the other now gripping my throat. His fingers dig into my skin and I can feel his breath on my face. He licks from my jawbone and up my cheek. "Maybe I need to fuck some sense into you, huh, Sugar, would you like that?"

"Please," I beg, fear coursing through my veins and for the first time since starting this undercover gig, I fear for my life.

He smirks, taking my plea as I want him, not that I want him to let me go. "You want my cock sliding into your cunt? Or maybe your mouth? Or if I remember correctly, you love a good ass fucking." He slides his hand from my hip to my ass, rubbing his finger along my ass crack, squeezing my asscheek roughly. The grip on my throat tightens. It's becoming hard to breathe, spots begin to dot my vision. "Is that what you want, Sugar? You want my cock in your ass while I finger your cunt?"

My eyes well with tears and fear bubbles throughout my body. I'm on the verge of passing out when he loosens his grip, but he's still choking me. "Please, Kye," I beg again. "I'm with you one-hundred-percent." I swallow deeply and fasten my gaze on him. I stare into his dead, evil black eyes. "I warned you about Creed. I warned you that he was unstable, and look, three days before the biggest meeting since you took over, your right-hand man gets arrested." He lets my throat go, and on instinct I lift my hand and rub. "I'm with you, Kye, one hundred and ten percent. I always have been and always will be. The fact you don't realize that, hurts. Maybe I'm not your queen after all."

Straightening my dress, I turn around, and with my head held high, I walk toward the exit. Once outside, I run over to my car. Unlocking the door, I climb in and grab my phone. I unlock it and send a message to the one person I need right now.

CHAPTER 14

Corey

MY PHONE PINGS WITH A TEXT. I drop my pen, pick it up, and unlock the screen. Opening my messages, I read.

> **BAYLOR**
>
> I need to see you.
>
> NOW!

I stare at her texts and that rumbling in my gut feeling from the other day returns with a vengeance. My fingers slide over the screen and I immediately text her back.

> **COREY**
>
> When and where?

> The apartment. Now.

> See you there.

Closing my laptop, I grab my things and race to the parking lot to drive over to Baylor and Avery's. She pulls up at the same time as I do, and I don't like the look on her face.

Climbing out, I yell, "Baylor!" She looks up at me and smiles, but it isn't her usual bright smile. Walking toward her, I stop in front of her but before I can speak, she says.

"I'm scared, Cox. I don't think I can do this. I…"

"Kitten," I cup her cheek, "I won't let anything happen to you." I pause "Do you trust me?" She nods her head. "Good, then trust me. Let's go upstairs and we can talk."

She nods again. Like a robot on autopilot, we head inside the building and up to the apartment. We enter and Baylor heads straight to the kitchen, she grabs a bottle of tequila, pulls off the cap, and chugs. She bites her lip and stares at nothing.

"Kitten, you're scaring me. What happened?" She looks at me, but doesn't say anything; her silence is unnerving. "Baylor!" I shout and that garners her attention.

"You called me Baylor."

"That's your name."

"You either call me Kitten or Ms. Evans." She pauses and bites her lip. "I really like the way you say my name. The way your tongue wraps around the 'lor' is refreshing."

"That's great but what's got you so freaked? We met not three hours ago."

"Kye, he, umm, he choked me." Her hand instinctively goes to her neck and she rubs it. "He…he threatened me."

"I'm pulling you out now. This is over."

"No!" she shouts, shaking her head. "I can do this. I just had to get out of there. I...I need...can...can you hold me?"

Without missing a beat, I step over to her and wrap my arms around her shoulders. She slides hers around my waist and holds on for dear life. Her body is shaking but all I can think about is how great she feels in my arms right now. She sniffles. "Are you crying?"

She shakes her head. "No, I think I'm allergic to you." She lifts her head and pushes away from me. Immediately, I feel the loss of her and I don't like it. We stare at one another. The air around us heating and sizzling, but the next words out of her mouth freeze me to my core. "I'll be at the meeting this Thursday by his side. As his queen."

"I said no." My voice is loud and takes on an authoritative tone.

"Well, he said I needed to be there and after being choked an hour ago, I'll be there." She lifts her hand to her neck and runs her fingers back and forth across her skin. She looks me dead in the eye and my Kitten's spark is back. "Deal with it, Cox." She continues to stare at me, her gaze egging me to snap and say something, but I refuse to give in to her. "What? Got nothing to say?" she taunts. "The Almighty Agent Cox is speechless. First time for everything." Just like that, sassy Baylor is back and truth be told, I now want to strangle her, after I sink myself balls deep inside of her.

She's always defying me. Pushing me but I still want her. Lifting my gaze back to hers and even though she's being tough right now, I see vulnerability and fear reflecting in her eyes.

"Kitten, what happened after you left here?"

She swallows deeply. She licks her lips and stares into nothing. "When I got to the warehouse, Monica was there. I really cannot stand that skank. She got my hackles up, and then Kye and I got into it. He demanded I be there. At first I refused, your words were ringing in my head, but he wasn't taking no for an answer. I relented." She pauses. "Then he asked if I was hiding something. I don't think I hesitated but Kye is good at reading people. He didn't like my answer and that's when he choked me. I managed to convince him I was Team Kye, we kissed and made up." I growl at hearing she kissed him again. "Down, boy, it's a figure of speech. I managed to get him back onside but I had to get out of there. I wanted to see you." She quietly adds, "I needed you."

"Are you okay?" This is a side of Baylor I've never seen before, she's normally ball-busting, taking shit from no one, but right now, she's the complete opposite of that.

She turns her gaze to me. "I'm ready for this to be over."

"After Thursday, it will be. Thankfully, we have time to work on you and your safety into the plan. Nothing will happen to you, I promise. We want Vlahos only. We will need to arrest you to keep up appearances, but I'll be the one to cuff you."

"Kinky," she teases, "I never picked you as a deviant but then again, it's always the ones you least expect." And just like that, my Kitten is back. She jumps up on the countertop and winks at me. My cock twitches when she does this. *What is this woman doing to me?* "Should I bring my own cuffs, or will you supply them?"

Suddenly, I get a vision of Baylor cuffed to my bed. She's wearing a sexy virginal white lace bra and panty set. She looks like an angel, but in reality, she's the devil in disguise. "Yo, Cox. Earth to Cox."

Her voice snaps me away from my dirty thoughts. "Sorry, what?" I reply like a loser.

"Where did you go just now?"

"Trying to work out the best way to keep you safe," I tell her, impressed with myself for coming up with the ruse so quickly.

"I will be safe, won't I?" She looks down at the floor, swinging her legs back and forth to keep herself grounded.

Placing my finger under her chin, I lift her gaze to mine. "I will do everything in my power to keep you safe, Kitten."

"I know you will," she quietly murmurs, giving me a small smile. Her voice is soft, something you don't often hear from the firecracker that is Baylor Evans.

We stare intently at one another. A force takes over my body and I step closer to her. Nudging her legs apart, I step between them and reach up to cup her cheek in my hand. She leans into my palm and nuzzles into it. Turning her head, she places a kiss on my skin. Her lips are warm and silky soft. She reaches up and cups my cheek like I did to her. I too turn my head and kiss her palm.

With our hands cupping each other's cheek, we continue to stare at one another, the temperature in the kitchen rising with each passing second. Our breathing becomes labored and my cock is already at half-mast and we haven't even done anything yet. Her tongue darts out and she licks her bottom lip then bites it. "Fuck it," I whisper.

Gripping both her cheeks in my palms, I press my lips to hers. She drapes her arms over my shoulders and pulls me into her, deepening our kiss and connection. She wraps her leg around my waist. I can feel the heat of her pussy. She moans into my mouth and my cock is now standing at full attention.

Sliding my hand down her body, her nipples pebble from my touch but I keep moving south. Pushing up the material of her dress, I slip my hand between her thighs and cup her mound. Her panties are soaked with her arousal. I rub her through the material as I continue to kiss her. Our tongues sliding in and out of each other's mouth's.

Pulling her panties to the side, I slide my finger between her lips and my eyes widen when I feel the metal ring on her clit. *I can't wait to play with that*, I think to myself as I push two fingers deep inside her.

"Cox," she mewls against my lips, as I continue to thrust my fingers in and out of her.

Pulling my lips away from hers, I watch as she falls apart. Her walls clench around my fingers and when I press my thumb against her clit, she cries out as she climaxes. She falls back against the countertop and rides out the rest of her release.

Removing my fingers, I bring them to my lips and lick her juices off them. "You have the sweetest tasting pussy, Kitten. A man could become addicted."

She sits up and stares at me. Without saying a word, she slides off the counter and drops to her knees. She lifts her hands and I watch as she undoes my belt, flicks open the button, and lowers the zipper of my slacks. She slips beneath the waistband and grips my cock in her tiny hand, squeezing and tugging as she pulls it out. The head is angry, purple, and dripping with precum. She licks her lips and with her eyes locked on mine, she opens her mouth and sucks me like a lollipop. Her tongue swirls around the tip before she swallows me whole. She opens her throat and takes me deep into her mouth.

"Your mouth is like heaven," I groan, threading my fingers into her hair. I guide her head back and forth. The image of her sucking my dick is so much better in reality. Much sooner than I would like, my balls begin to tingle. "I'm about to come," I incoherently mumble, this is the best BJ in history of BJs. Her head bobs faster, my legs stiffen, and I come down her throat. She grips my asscheeks and sucks every last drop from me.

My cock pops out of her mouth, and she wipes at the corner, seductively sucking her finger. "Mmmmm," she moans.

Standing up, she stares into my eyes. I know I should feel bad about what just happened since I'm her handler but I don't. What does surprise me is her reaction. "I think you should go. I need to focus," she says. "I need you to go."

Cutting her off, I put my finger to her lips and nod. "I'll go. Baylor—"

"You called me Baylor, again," she says.

"That is your name."

She shakes her head, "You said that earlier too—" The moment is interrupted when the front door opens, "Bay, I'm home!" Avery yells out.

"Shit," I curse. I jump back and quickly put my cock away and rezip my pants.

Baylor laughs and sings out, "In here." My eyes widen at her response. Just as I've fixed my pants, Avery steps into the kitchen.

"Ohh, hi, Agent Cox."

"Corey is just fine and hello to you too, Ms. Evans."

"Well, if I can call you Corey, you can call me Avery."

"Hi, Avery," I say to her before turning to face Baylor. She's sitting back up on the counter, swinging her legs back and forth without a care in the world. She's grinning like the cat who caught the canary, me being the canary. She raises her eyebrows at me in that smart-ass way I'm coming to love. "Kitten, I'll be in touch once I have a plan formulated. Stay safe."

Reaching out, I squeeze her knee. We stare at each other for a few heartbeats and then I turn around to leave. Smiling at Avery on my way past, I exit the apartment and let out a deep breath.

Climbing into my car, I lean my head back and close my eyes. What the fuck have I just done?

CHAPTER 15
Baylor

"SOOO, HOW WAS YOUR DAY?" Ave teases, jumping up onto the counter next to me. She rests her head on my shoulder and I lean into her. I think about her question and internally laugh. Today has been crazy and chaotic, just another day in the life of Bailey Martine Evans.

"Long. Interesting. Frightening." *Erotic*, I silently add. "Take your pick."

She lifts her head and turns to look at me, her face etched with worry. I know these past few months have been tough on her but I'm happy she has Flynn. I'm glad that my actions didn't ruin that for her. Apart from the worry, I haven't see her happy like this in a very long time. "Why was it frightening?" She reaches over and squeezes my hand in that concerned sisterly way. Looking down at our joined hands, I take a deep breath and I tell her everything that transpired today.

"You gave him a blow job in our kitchen?"

"That's what you are focusing on with regard to everything that I just said?"

"I'll circle back to the rest. I want to know how you go from formulating a plan to bring down a drug kingpin to both of you going down on one another?"

"This is me, why are you surprised?"

"Touché." She nods, "So how did it happen?"

"Well, my mouth sucked his dick like it was a lollipop and he ate my vagina like a starved man."

"Crass much, Bay?"

"What can I say, Cress is rubbing off on me."

"More like you were rubbing one off on him."

"Avery Evans, I have never heard you speak so crassly before, I'm impressed."

"What can I say, Cress is rubbing off on me." We both laugh. "But seriously, Bay, how did that happen? I thought you hated him?"

"I do, he's a straitlaced dick with a stick up his ass. Always doing the right thing. Always riding my ass but…"

"But what?"

"But I can't stop thinking about him. He's fucking hot in that suit and his dick, fuck, Ave, it's the most beautiful one I've ever seen."

"Dicks are ugly."

"Not this one," I say, a goofy grin on my face as I think back to his dick in my hand and mouth.

"Okay, so he's hot with a beautiful dick and he pisses you off. Sounds like the start of a beautiful love story to me."

"Pffft, I never said I was in love with him."

"No, but you are falling for him."

I've already fallen, I silently say. "Doesn't matter, we can never be. We are too different."

"Flynn and I are different."

"We are different in that I'm a lawbreaker and he's a lawmaker. Can't get more different than that."

"You're not a criminal."

"Tell that to my record," I snap at Ave, my voice harsher than I intended but regardless, Corey and I can never be. "I just need to finish this thing and then forget I ever met Corey Cox."

"If that's what you want but for what it's worth, I don't think that is what you want."

A laugh escapes me, "Ave, I don't know what I want."

"There's plenty of time to figure it out." We both fall silent and I think about what she said. However, time is not my friend, if this all goes to plan, by the end of the week this case will be wrapped up, and Corey will move onto the next case, and I'll be off to jail.

Ave jumps off the counter and breaks the silence, "It's Wine Wednesday, let's see if we can come up with a plan over a bottle of red."

"Ave, I don't think wine will fix this but I'm happy to give it a shot."

"No, we don't shoot wine, we sip it and savor it."

"I'm not posh, Ave. Hell, give me a wine box, a straw, and I'm good to go."

She snort-laughs as she reaches into the wine fridge, grabbing a bottle of red, while I jump down and grab two glasses. She opens the bottle and pours two generous glasses. Handing me mine, her face shines brightly. "Cheese, we need cheese."

"Yes, nothing beats wine and cheese."

Like a well-oiled machine, Ave and I put together a kick-ass cheese platter. With our wine and platter in hand, we head into the living room. We both sit down and in sync, we tuck our legs under ourselves and snuggle back. I look over at Ave and realize she and I are in a good place. "I'm glad we're back on track," I tell her.

"Me too," she says. "I thought I'd lost you there for a while, but who knew that a mafia drug dude would bring us back together?"

"At least Kye is good for something." Taking a sip, I sigh.

"It's a good vintage, hey?" Ave says, mistaking my dejected sigh as a sigh of appreciation for the cab merlot.

"It is, but that's not what the sigh was for."

"Wanna talk about it?"

"What's there to talk about?"

"Whatever's bothering you."

"I…I feel…"

Ave leans forward and places her glass on the coffee table, then she scoots closer to me, and takes my hand in hers. She squeezes it reassuringly. "Bay, let it all out. Just spew the words; maybe you don't need advice. Maybe you just need to get it all out."

"Spew the words, so eloquent." She eyes me in that mom/teacher way and I think, *Fuck it.* Taking a huge gulp of wine I purge it all out. "I'm scared that once this is all over, I'm going to get into trouble again. I'm annoyed Kye isn't who I thought he was, and I'm sad that come Thursday, I'll never see Corey again. You're right, I *have* fallen for the straitlaced sexy agent but because I'm me, we can never be. And I'm concerned that when I do my time, I'm going to fall into the wrong crowd and be led astray again. I don't want to turn into Bitchy Baylor again. I want to be Badass Brilliant Baylor."

"Do you want advice? Or were you just venting?"

"Will I like the advice you give me?"

She shrugs at me and makes a face. "Just then you remind me of Porky from *The Little Rascals* when he shrugs."

"I made Flynn watch that recently, he'd never seen it before."

"What? How can he not have seen that movie?"

"I know, right? I rectified that...with red wine and sexy naked times."

"Avery Evans, you dirty, dirty girl...I'm so proud of you, joining the dirty side."

"You sound like Cress. She called me skank-hopper the weekend I met Flynn."

"Skank-hopper, I love that." I look to Ave, "Okay, yes, I do want advice. What do you have for me?"

"Step one. Drink more wine." She leans forward, tops up our glasses, and hands me mine. After she settles back into the sofa, she looks at me. "It's one thing at a time. First, bring down Kye and get rid of him. Put him in the 'later mater, nice knowing you' pile. Then you do your time. Twelve months isn't all that long. When you get out, look up Agent Cox and see what fate has to say."

"So I basically leave it up to fate then?"

"Pretty much. If it's meant to be with Cox, it will be."

"Well, that's not an easy fix."

"Life isn't easy, Bay, and the sooner you realize that, the sooner you'll find your own happiness."

"When did you get so wise?"

"I've always been wise."

"No one likes a gloater."

She sticks out her tongue at me and I can't help but laugh. Taking a sip of my wine, I think about what she said. This path to redemption is long and arduous, there's no quick fix. I wonder if I will ever get my happily ever after? Or if I'm destined to be alone for life since I'm such a screw up. Whether it be with Cox or someone I haven't met yet, I hope it's not too late for me.

CHAPTER 16

Corey

TODAY IS the day I bring down Kye Vlahos and rather than excitement for this, I'm upset that today will be the last time I see Baylor. That woman has wormed her way into my heart. Her frustrating, snarky, foul mouth has grown on me. A knock on my door snaps my head up and I smile. "Charli Davis, what the hell are you doing here?" I say as I walk over to her and wrap my arms around her.

"Dean and I are here finalizing the details for the Underdown trial."

"Bet you'll be glad to see the backend of that case. It was a never-ending shitshow."

"Tell me about it. Thankfully, the ducks were finally in a row and the case closed itself. Now we can hand Underdown over to the prosecution and we can move on to the next case."

"Any idea on what that is?"

"Nah, not yet but I'm sure the next person needing protection will be just as lovely as him."

Charli and I went through the academy together. If ever I were to work with a partner, it would be her. She's a ball-buster but she gets the job done. She's the best WitSec handler there is. She's never lost a witness under her watch.

"Got time for a coffee?" I ask her.

"Sure, Dean is catching up with a detective buddy of his, so I've got a few."

"Sweet." We walk toward to break room and I fill her in on the Vlahos case, leaving out my feelings, or whatever they are, for Baylor Evans. Just as we've sat down, her partner, Dean Chikatilo, walks up to us. "Let's roll," he rudely says, ignoring me. I'm not a fan of his and the feeling is mutual. Dean is a cowboy, how Charli puts up with him is beyond me but they seem to work well together.

She looks up. "Sure, give me a sec," she says to him. Looking back to me, she smiles. It's a megawatt Charli smile. "Good luck with the Vlahos takedown today. Seems your risky plan using Evans was a good move."

"I'm hurt you ever doubted me." I fake offense and she laughs.

"Everyone doubted you, Cox," Dean snarls, his gaze locked on me. "Using a junkie as your way in was stupid and fucked up, if you ask me."

"Not me," Charli interrupts, breaking the tension. "I was rooting for you and knew you could do it."

"Of course you were," Dean says, rolling his eyes. "Let's go." He turns and walks out without a goodbye.

"Bye, Dean," I quietly quip at his retreating form.

Charli laughs, "Thanks for the coffee. We should do drinks soon."

"A proper catch-up sounds good," I tell her.

"Awesome, let me know when and where. Later, Corey." She stands and walks out but pops her head back in. "For what it's worth, I would have done the same thing as you. You've got this, but good luck."

Before I can reply, she's gone again. Sitting here, I stare into my mug and shake my head. The end is here and rather than focusing on the game plan for today, I keep thinking about her. If I lose focus, everything I've worked toward is going to come crashing down and it will all be for nothing. I need to put Baylor Evans out of my mind and focus. My goal is to bring down Kye Vlahos and see him behind the bars for the rest of his life, not get the girl...but is there a way to do both?

CHAPTER 17
Baylor

MY MIND IS all over the place today. I'm so nervous I want to vomit. Kye keeps staring at me and it's making my skin crawl. I wish I could hug Ave one last time because I have a feeling that after today, I'm never going to see her again. We said our goodbyes this morning after our wine and movie night. Not only did we watch *The Little Rascals*, we also watched *Ten Things I Hate About You* and *Empire Records*. We stayed up later than called for mid-week, but it was what Ave and I, especially me, needed. When she left for work this morning, we hugged each other tighter than usual. I was glad when she said she'd be with Flynn for the next few days. With everything that's about to go down, I don't want her anywhere near the apartment...or me.

Kye growling my name snaps me back to the present. I shake my head, trying to clear the fog. "Sorry, what?"

"Where's your head at? You've been aloof for the last few days."

"Just tired," I offer with a smile that's one-million-percent fake than fake smile. "Didn't sleep much last night."

"You worried, Sugar?"

Nodding my head, I decide to go with honesty. "Yes, I am. I don't want to be there today—" he goes to interrupt but I stand up, walk over to him, and press my finger to his lips, "but I promised I would and as your queen, I'll be there. Not sure what my presence will accomplish but a promise is a promise."

"And that's why you're my queen." The anger from the other day is gone and replaced is the arrogant egotistical Kye Vlahos that we all know and hate. "You know, you can have a more active role if you wish. I'd give you anything, Baylor." He cups my cheek in a loving way. "One day, I hope we can get back to where we were before I set all of this in motion. Sugar, I know my death affected you and I'm sorry I did that but at the same time, I'm not because now…now I can give you the world. After today, the city will be ours. I want to share and bask in this glory with you."

Staring at him, my heart begins to race; this feels like a do-or-die moment. You know that moment in the movie when it's all about to change, that's what this feels like, but in reality, the decision is not so easy to make. With what's being offered, the old me would have jumped at the chance to be Queen Bitch: ruler of the city with minions at my beck and call. Without blinking, I would have shoved anyone in my way to the side and stomped on them. The new me, however, she's hesitant but Kye is literally offering me the world and that's kind of hard to resist.

He grips my chin and lifts my gaze to his. He stares intently at me and something passes between us. My hatred toward him begins to thaw. Those feelings from before surface and slam into me like a tidal wave. My heart begins to beat faster. My skin heating at his touch. "Will you rule by my side? Be the queen you were born to be?"

Without any hesitation, I whisper, "Yes, I'll be your queen and together we will rule this city." As those words pass my mouth, a sinister smile appears on my face. With this decision made, I feel freer than I have in weeks. Bring. It. On.

When my words register, Kye, too, smiles. It sends shivers down my spine. He cups my cheek, "The city will be ours, My Queen." But like everything that is in my life, it all comes crashing down.

CHAPTER 18

Corey

TO SAY today was a clusterfuck is the understatement of the fucking century. I should have trusted my gut but no, I went with my heart and it nearly cost me everything.

Leaning back in my chair, I replay everything that happened in the last five hours...

...It's go time. My team and I are doing the final preparations before we leave to take down Kye Vlahos. Baylor has been silent for the last few days, and I have a sneaking suspicion that she's going to screw me over...and it's all because of me and my actions. After our last meeting, when things happened that should never have happened, it blurred the lines between us. I think it pushed things too far. There's a feeling deep in the pit of my stomach, yelling to me that something is amiss. And then there's my head, thinking about Baylor and her gorgeous fucking lips wrapped around my dick. And finally, we have my heart. It's beating with little love hearts for the blonde bombshell, who can never be anything more than my informant...and someone who gave me the best blow job of my life.

Shaking my head, I slip on my vest and look to my team. Charli and Dean are joining us since they are between cases. I'm happy to have them along with us because we need all the manpower we can.

Everyone's eyes are on me. "Let's do this," I declare to the team. "Our main objective is to bring Kye Vlahos to justice. If we can nab his cronies or those whom he's meeting with too, then great, but Vlahos is our main target. Baylor Evans needs to be kept safe if possible, she's been a great help in gathering this intel and I'd hate to see her hurt or killed."

"You sure we can trust the bitch?" Dean asks.

My hackles rise when he refers to her as a bitch. "Yes, we can. She hasn't indicated otherwise."

"That's not what Creed Dawson says."

"Why were you talking with him?"

"It doesn't concern you." His response doesn't sit well with me but I don't have time to dwell on him, or Dawson.

"Let's get in and out and hope that it's smooth."

"You just jinxed that," Charli adds, shaking her head as she fastens her vest.

"Wanna bet on it?"

"You bet. Less than five casualties, it's my shout. Anything above five, and it's your shout."

"You're on, Davis," I tell her, outstretching my hand to shake on it.

"You're going down, Cox."

After we seal our bet—with the others making bets of their own —we all file out and climb into the van. Looking around, I trust eight of the nine agents and officers in here. My eyes are locked on Dean, I hate that fucker but he's Charli's partner. She wouldn't work with someone she doesn't trust, and I trust her with my life so I have to trust he has our backs too.

We pull up across the road from the meeting, it's being held at a restaurant in Little Italy just off Sheridan Park. We watch as multiple crime bosses along the East Coast enter the restaurant one by one. If we can take them all down, it will be a great win for us, and a huge hit to the drug and trafficking trade on the East Coast.

A car with tinted windows pulls up and I know she's here. The door opens and a long slender leg appears and then she climbs out. She's a fucking knockout at the best of times but today, fuck me sideways, she looks like a queen. She's wearing sky-high black heels and a figure-hugging purple dress that accentuates each and every delectable curve. The neckline plunges and showcases her tits spectacularly. She walks around the back of the sedan and joins Vlahos on the sidewalk. He says something to her and she smiles at him. The look she gives him lights up her face and it hits me straight in the balls. A groan emits in the back of my throat. Charli looks at me questioningly and Dean, the fucking dick, smirks and not so subtly readjusts his cock.

Vlahos slips his arm around her waist and the two of them walk inside, along with his henchmen.

Grabbing my laptop, I log into the app for the recorder installed on Baylor's phone, and wait for it to connect. It's staticky at first and then I hear his voice and what he says has me clenching my fist and grinding my molars, that is until Baylor replies. "Kye, we are here to discuss business not how fucking fabulous I look.

Everyone in this room knows I'm hot and in a few moments, they will feel my wrath if they don't stop eye fucking me, you included. Now, everyone take their fucking seats and let's get started."

"She's a firecracker," Charli says, and I find myself nodding.

"You have no clue, Davis."

Chuckles erupt from my team, most of them were there the day Baylor was brought in and I floated this plan with the captain. They all thought I was crazy, hell, most of them still think I'm crazy, but if this all goes down how I hope today, my crazy plan will have paid off.

"When are we going in, boss?" Coombs asks.

"Let's wait and see what this meeting is all about. Plus, backup is still not here."

"Cox will know when," Charli says. "His instinct is always on point."

Looking to Charli, I nod. I'm glad she's here today; she will ground me and keep me in line. Her faith in me restores my confidence this will work out. Heat sensors show they are all congregated in the back of the restaurant in the large private dining room, making our entrance that much easier and more of a surprise.

Kye introduces everyone to his queen, and now that the introductions have been made, they start discussing business. Kye really is a piece of shit, someone in that room might take him out before we get in there.

All eyes are on me, awaiting the go signal. Backup still isn't here but I don't want to miss my chance. I have a good team, minus

Dean, so I make the decision to move. "Remember, Vlahos is the main target. Anyone else we detain is a bonus and don't forget, Baylor Evans is technically one of ours."

Everyone nods in agreement and with that, it's time for me and my team to make our presence known. "Let's move."

The ten of us file out of the van. Two head left, two head right. The restaurant has no back access so that makes things easier for us. The remaining five and I head toward the front entrance. Dean is the first to shoot when two men exit the restaurant. He pops them both off, one after the other. He looks at me in that smarmy 'you're welcome' way.

"That's two," Charli says with a wink, as she and Dean fall into sync and enter the restaurant before me. Following each other's lead, I notice they work well together. Stepping over the bodies Dean dropped, I enter the behind them.

We fan out and approach the rooms at the back. My heart is racing. I've been involved in many sting operations but this one is the first time where I'm nervous and on edge. Our plan is rock-solid; the only variable is Baylor-fucking-Evans.

The teams outside radio in and tell us they are in place, they are our backup in case Vlahos escapes. There are two entrances into the room, which is perfect for us. Looking at everyone, I raise my hand and indicate on three. I flick up one finger and when all three are up, I indicate it's go time.

Raising my leg, I kick open the door and step into the room.

"What the fuck?" Vlahos snarls, just as the back door to the room is also kicked in. The six of us have our guns pointed toward him. There are eight men sitting down, plus Baylor. Kye is standing at the head of the table; his face is laced with shock

right now. He draws his weapon as he steps over to Baylor and places his hand on her shoulder. He squeezes it, she looks up at him lovingly, and that one look guts me. He leans down and presses a kiss to her temple. It seems the prick really does care about her, or it's a ploy and he'll use her to protect himself. But from the look she's giving him in return, it seems like she cares for him too. I'm really hoping that it's all an act. That she's a really good actress and playing the doting girlfriend role.

Snapping my attention back to him, I clear my throat. "Kye Vlahos, you are under arrest for drug trafficking, human trafficking, and murder."

"Like you have shit on me, pig," he spits at me. "I suggest you turn around and walk out of here. That way we can pretend you didn't just interrupt this reunion, and everyone can go on their merry way."

All eyes in the room are flicking between the two of us. My gaze keeps dropping to Baylor but I try and maintain eye contact with Vlahos. "Yeah, that's not going to happen. Now we can do this the easy way, or the hard way. Choice is yours."

"I'm going to have so much fun," Kye says, his voice a sinister tone and I know that this is all about to turn to shit, and shit is an understatement. Kye pulls the trigger and that sets off a chain reaction of gunfire. Even through all the gunfire, I hear Baylor's screams.

Without thinking, I rush forward but I'm stopped when Vlahos raises his arm and presses the barrel of his gun to my head. On instinct, I raise my arm and point my pistol at him. Each of us staring the other down. The room falls silent; all eyes are on us. Baylor crawls out from under the table. She stands up and when she turns around, she gasps in shock. Her eyes dart back and forth between us.

A lone gunshot cracks through the air. My eyes widen and the next moments are played out in an ultraslow motion. Baylor screams as Vlahos falls to the floor, clutching his shoulder. Baylor drops to her knees and presses her hand to his shoulder. "Kye, no-no-no," she cries, tears cascading down her cheeks. She isn't faking her concern for him. She looks over the table and stares at someone. Turning my head, I see Dean standing there, arms still outstretched. He has a smirk on his face and then he pulls the trigger again. I feel the bullet fly past my head with millimeters to spare and a grunt emanates from behind me.

Turning my head, I see one of Vlahos' henchmen fall to the ground at my feet. A knife slipping out of his hand as his lifeless eyes stare up at me. A bullet hole in the center of his forehead.

"You shot him," Baylor cries over and over. Her hands are covered in blood when they come back up, an agent pulls her away kicking and screaming. They cuff her and that's when she really lets loose. "Get the fuck off me," she screams, "you fucking dicks."

I growl as I walk over to her, she's using excessive language right now but I guess it plays into her cover.

"Fuck you," she spits at me "Fuck you all."

Kye groans and her eyes snap to his. "Help him, you fuckers. He's been shot."

Her concern for him pisses me off. "Get her out of here," I tell the officer who cuffed her. He nods at me and without a word, escorts a still screaming Baylor out of here.

Walking over to Kye, I drop to my knees. "Seems your day didn't quite go as planned."

"You are a fucking dead man. You hear me? You're fucking dead."

"We'll see about that." A paramedic arrives and Kye is placed on the stretcher and cuffed to the bed rail. He's escorted out of here with two officers. I look around at the carnage. We lost two agents today. With the two outside and the one in here, a total of five people lost their lives, but we arrested Vlahos and all eight of his guests.

Kye is wheeled past and I taunt him, "Don't drop the soap."

He flips me the bird and is escorted out of the restaurant.

"Great job," Charli says to me as she leans against the table. "You got him."

Nodding my head in agreement, I remind, "We got him."

"Then why do you look like your kitten just died?"

My head snaps up at her choice of words because it does feel like my kitten died. She was absolutely distraught over Kye and that cuts me to the core, more than I would like to admit. Not wanting to discuss this, I go with the obvious answer. "Paperwork."

"Ugh, paperwork," she says, nodding her head. "So it seems after all the paperwork," she whispers the word paperwork, "you owe me a night out."

"It seems I do but you totally cheated."

"How so?"

"Your partner killed three of them, you had inside help."

"Yes, because Dean and I colluded together for me to win a night out at your expense."

"See, I knew it." We both laugh. "How about I finish this paperwork back at the office and tonight we head out."

"Sounds good to me."

We both exit the restaurant and head back to the precinct.

…and that brings me to now.

The paperwork is completed. All my I's dotted and all my T's are crossed. Kye Vlahos is behind bars and will be for a very long time. I should be over the moon that this is over, but all I feel is sadness at never seeing Baylor again. By the time I got back to the precinct, she'd already been processed and was on her way to The Metropolitan Correctional Center.

I will never see Baylor Evans again, and that upsets me more than it should.

CHAPTER 19

Baylor

CLIMBING OUT OF THE CAR, I can feel eyes on me—Cox is here. It's comforting knowing he is but at the same time, I'm shit fucking scared for what's about to transpire. Stepping onto the sidewalk, I look up and see Kye eye fucking me. My body heats from the intensity of his gaze. I smile seductively at him. He steps to me and slides his hand around my waist. "Fuck, you are a vision. My cock is throbbing at the sight of you in this dress."

"Well, let's get this over with and then…" I don't finish that sentence because there will be no after if all goes according to the plan. Kye licks his lips and we make our way inside. I look over my shoulder and up at the sky. It's clear blue, not a cloud in sight. Taking a deep breath, I hope I will see daylight again.

We enter the dark and dimly lit restaurant and a feeling of dread develops in the pit of my stomach, but I push it aside and follow Kye into a banquet room in the back. As soon as we enter, all conversation stops. Every head turns to face us. All eyes roam over me as if I'm a piece of meat. I remember the time Kye called, demanding I dress like a whore, and I smile at how far we've come. I look to him and I see the power emitting from him. He was born to lead. He's thriving as the head of the Vlahos family and if today goes according to plan, he will be THE head honcho of the East Coast. Watch out world, Kye-fucking-Vlahos is coming. But then I wonder, can I stand by him and watch what he does? The drugs I can handle, but it's the human trafficking and the murder I can't deal with.

He slides his hand around my waist and I'm snapped back to the present. He squeezes my hip in a possessive way and it reminds me of Cox the other night when he pushed me back to the counter and went down on me. I shudder at the memory and clench my thighs to ease the throb.

Fuck, how can I be thinking of that, and him, right now?

Looking over to Kye, I focus on him. "Gentleman, I give you Baylor Evans. My. Queen. Isn't she gorgeous?"

A murmur of agreements and head nods come from the men before us. *Pussies,* I think to myself as I raise my hand to silence them. "Kye, we are here to discuss business, not how fucking fabulous I look. Everyone in this room knows I'm hot and in a few moments, they will feel my wrath if they don't stop eye fucking me," turning to face Kye, I add, "you included. Now, everyone take their fucking seats and let's get started."

Pulling away from him, I take my seat, lean back and look around the room. These eight men are the evilest of the evil and each one of them deserves everything that will be coming through that door any moment now. I sit and listen to Kye ramble on and I come to the realization that he is just as evil as them, if not more so. He killed his own family to get where he is, there's nothing more despicable than that. I wonder if he will do that to me too, if I piss him off?

"My queen has a point," Kye says, leaning on the table. "We are here because I have a proposition for you all. As you know, I have recently taken over as head of the Vlahos family—"

"Rumor has it," a man to my left interrupts, "you killed them, including your own mother, to get this position of power. I speak for myself when I say, I'm not comfortable with that."

"And what proof do you have for this rumor?" Kye asks him pointedly. He's met with silence. "Exactly. It's all hearsay."

"Then why did you fake your death?" another asks.

"Because I didn't want to end up dead like them."

The room falls silent as everyone processes his words or should I say lies. For crooks, I can't believe they cannot smell the bullshit coming from Kye's mouth right now. *Fucking idiots.*

Before any more can be said, the door to the room is kicked open. The cracking of the wood startles me and Kye growls, "What the fuck?" Just as the other door is also kicked in. His eyes widen as six agents storm into the room. All six of them ignore every other person in the room and have their guns pointed toward Kye.

A hand squeezes my shoulder and when I look up, I see Kye, too, has his gun drawn. A fake smile is still on my face, and he glances down at me and winks. He thinks this is all a joke. I'm scared shitless right now but I cannot remove the smile from my face. I'm frozen with fear.

At the sound of Cox's voice, I turn my head and stare at him. He's all decked out in his combat gear and holy fucking hotness, Batman. A man in uniform is hot, but a man in combat gear, fuck, it sets my insides ablaze. He's focused on Kye and from next to me, I can feel the anger and rage building within Kye. He's on the edge, one wrong move and this is going to end in a gunfight, I don't have a good feeling for Cox and his team.

Kye antagonizes Cox. "Like you have shit on me, pig. I suggest you turn around and walk out of here. That way we can pretend you didn't just interrupt this reunion, and everyone can go on their merry way."

The room is silent, except for the heavy breathing of every person. Everyone's eyes are darting between Kye and Cox. The barbs are tossed back and forth between the two of them and when Kye's tone turns sinister, I begin to inch toward the front of my seat. Ready to drop and hide. I didn't sign up for this and if I die today, I will be coming back to haunt Corey Cox for the rest of his days.

I'm not sure who fires first but after that first shot, a symphony of gunfire follows. Grunts and bodies collapse all around me. I'm not sure if they are dropping from being shot or from hiding.

Dropping to the floor, I cover my head and crawl under the table. Curling into a ball, I make myself as small as possible. Someone is screaming and then I realize, it's me.

Fear courses through my veins. My is heart racing, beating loud and fast in my ears.

Opening my eyes, I see legs moving but they stop suddenly and the room falls silent. A few seconds ago, it was chaos, and now, nothing. Taking a few deep breaths, I crawl out from under the table and when my eyes land on the standoff between Kye and Cox, I gasp in shock. I don't want either one of them to get hurt, but I know that one of them will not be walking out of here alive.

It all happens so fast, yet at the same time, so slow. Kye drops to the ground, clutching his shoulder. His eyes wide open with shock. Dropping to my knees, I crawl over to him. "Kye, no-no-no," I cry, as I press my hand to the bullet wound. Deep red blood stains his shirt. I've never seen blood up close before, it's definitely not like it is in the movies.

Lifting my head, I glance over the table and I see an agent with his arms raised. My eyes widen as realization hits that he's going to kill Cox. My heart begins to race at the thought of Cox getting shot. He pulls the trigger, and I wait for Cox to collapse to the ground but to my surprise, one of Kye's men grunts and drops to the ground before me.

His eyes are vacant, staring into nothing. A trickle of blood drips down his nose from the single bullet hole in the center of his forehead.

Kye groans and my attention snaps back to him. Gently I lift his head and cradle it in my lap. Over and over I repeat, "You shot him." My cries becoming louder and louder. Someone grips my arms and lifts me into a standing position. Kye's head drops to the blood-stained carpet and he grunts again. My arms are twisted behind my back and I'm cuffed.

"Get the fuck off me," I scream and wriggle, "you fucking dicks."

I try to pull free of the officer but he's got me cuffed and in his grasp. I look at Cox; I want nothing more than to hug him, but as Ave reminded me, I need to pretend I don't know him. So I spit at him and growl, "Fuck you. Fuck you all."

Kye moans and my eyes drop to him. He deserves everything that's coming but no one deserves to be in pain, I'm guessing getting shot hurts like a bitch. "Help him, you fuckers. He's been shot," I cry again. "Please," I beg. "Help him."

Tears pour down my face as the adrenaline pumping around my body begins to fade. Lifting my gaze, my eyes meet Corey's but I don't see the man who cares about me. I don't see the man who made me come on his face the other day. All I see is a straitlaced professional agent.

The final knife to my heart is when I hear him say. "Get her out of here." Those five words hurt like a sledgehammer.

He won't meet my gaze and it seems he really did only want me for my help to get Kye. He doesn't care about me at all. I stupidly thought after the other night that when this was all over, we could try something but I guess, I was wrong.

The officer escorts me out of the restaurant and into an awaiting cruiser. I'm taken to the station and placed into a holding room. I hated being in this room a few months ago and I hate it even now. It's so cold and sterile. The door opens and a female officer walks in. "Baylor Evans?" she asks. It's on the tip of my tongue to say no and be a snarky bitch but I just nod at her. "You're being transferred in ten."

"Where's Cox?" I ask her.

"Not here. I will be processing your transfer to MCC."

"What the fuck is MCC?"

"The Metropolitan Correctional Center. It will be home for the next," she looks at the file in her hand, "twelve months for you, Ms. Evans."

"Can I see my sister before we go?"

She shakes her head, "I'm afraid not. Details will be passed on to your family regarding visitation in the coming weeks."

"Weeks?" I shout, my eyes well with tears at the thought of not seeing or speaking to Ave for a few weeks. "I need my sister," I blubber.

"I'm sorry."

"Well, can I see Cox then?"

"As I said, he's not here. If I see him, I'll let him know but he's currently out in the field."

"I fucking know that," I snap. "I was with him when this all went down. Don't you know who I am? What I did for you people?" I know I'm being a bitch right now, but this is all happening too fast. I knew it was going to happen but knowing and reality are two different things.

"Curb the language and your attitude, Ms. Evans. I'll be back to collect you soon."

The door closes and I mumble, "Fucking bitch." Her words remind me of Cox and I smile to myself. *Fucking Cox.*

Resting my head on the table, I sigh in defeat and begin to cry again. I did all of this for my freedom. Forgetting that before I get my freedom, I'll be locked away. Tears cascade down my cheeks as the reality of it all sets in. I'm upset I can't say goodbye to Ave. That I can't tell her my plan to cozy up to Kye and be his queen worked. I'm sad I won't get to see Corey again. That I can't see the joy on his face at getting the bad guy. That I won't get to kiss him again or sleep with him. I know we are different but we could work, if we tried.

Sitting up, I lean back in my chair and whisper, "Falling for Agent Cox was fucking stupid. I will never fall for a man again, it hurts too much when it turns to shit."

CHAPTER 20

Corey

...twelve months later

A KNOCK at my door has me lifting my head and grinding my teeth at the interruption. That anger is put aside when I see the captain at my door. "Captain," I say in greeting. "What can I do for you?"

He walks in and takes a seat. From the look on his face, I know it's not going to be good. "I have some news," he tells me.

"Okay." His demeanor is scaring me. I begin to think that something has happened to Mom and Dad but if it were in regard to them, Aunt Bec would have called me.

"It's Vlahos," he says, his tone unnerving.

"What about the asshole?" His lawyer has been a douchebag this last twelve months. He's tried to have the charges dismissed multiple times but I have an ironclad case, and each time the DA and I get their motion for dismissal denied.

"He escaped."

"What the fuck," I shout. "How the fuck did that happen?"

"He was taken to hospital with suspected appendicitis and with the help of his associates on the outside, he escaped. He killed two officers and severely injured a nurse."

"Fuck me." Rubbing my forehead in frustration, I glance up and from the look on his face I can tell there's more. "Just spit the rest out."

"Creed Dawson was found dead in his cell a few moments ago."

"Fuck me," I groan, "and let me guess, it looks like a suicide but you and I both know it's not."

"Not this time, Cox. He was definitely murdered." He's still shuffling and I just know there's more. I wish he'd just spit to out.

"Why do I feel like there's more?"

"Because there is," he confirms.

"Shit comes in threes," I tell him, "What's the third shitastic news you have for me?"

"A note was found near Dawson's body. It was addressed to you and let's just say, it's very concerning."

"What did it say?"

"It said, 'Rats like to squeal. You and that bitch are going down.'"

"What bitch?" But as soon as I voice it, I know exactly who Vlahos is referring to, Baylor Evans.

"I'm guessing he's discovered Ms. Evans was helping you."

"Baylor-fucking-Evans, I thought I was rid of her," I tell him, but it's a lie, a big fucking lie. She's been on my mind every single day for the last twelve months. Hell, I even dream about her and have woken up on several occasions with a rock-hard dick. I'd either have to take a cold shower or whack one out just so I could get back to sleep. "Where is she right now?"

"Funny you should ask, she was released from prison today. The timing is quite the coincidence, if you ask me."

"Is she aware of the threat made?"

"Not as yet. I came to see you to get your opinion on what we do from here."

"Me? Why do I care what happens?"

"Because she was your informant. I thought—"

"No, no, I get it. I'll reach out to her and tell her to be careful."

"Maybe you should put someone on her. Just to be safe."

"I'm sure it'll all be fine. Let's just find this fucker and put him back where he belongs."

"Corey, you need to be careful, too. Don't go all cowboy on this."

"You first named me, you really are concerned."

"When a threat is made against one of my agents, you bet your fucking ass I'm concerned. Now, I want you to arrange surveillance for Ms. Evans and you need to go see her and give her a heads-up."

"Fine," I relent. "I'll get on it after I finish this report."

"Now, Cox. The timing of all of this is too much of a coincidence. My gut is telling me this is going to turn to shit and as I said, I refuse to lose an agent or informant."

The look on his face doesn't give me any room to negotiate, so I nod my head and begin to pack up, looks like I'll be seeing Ms. Evans once again.

CHAPTER 21
Baylor

TODAY IS the start of my new life…or so they say.

Today I'm being released from jail for my part in the drug sting. I'm not the same person I was when I first went in. Hell, I'm not the person I was before I went undercover. I'd heard stories that prison changes a person. I thought they were full of shit but once again, I was mistaken.

Don't get me wrong; I'm still a bitch. But now, I'm a lovable one. I still love all things purple and bagels with cream cheese are still THE best food items ever created in the history of foods…and grape taffy is life. But now, I have a future. I actually care about my future and have dreams. I want to work in a bar and I want to become a mixologist. I'm also looking forward to spending some time with Ave and her soon-to-be fiancé—that is if she says yes tonight.

Flynn came to visit me the other week. I was shocked when I walked into the visitors' room and saw him alone. At first I thought Ave was in the bathroom but when it became clear she wasn't, my thoughts turned to the worst. She was dead, or sick, or she was abducted by aliens. Thankfully, she was fine—no alien anal probing for her— and he was here to ask, well, tell me, he was going to propose. I squealed in delight, garnering odd looks from the guards, inmates, and their visitors.

Flynn really is the perfect person for my sister, sure they are polar opposites but as the saying goes 'opposites attract.' I nearly ruined that for them when I was in over my head, but I'm glad my meddling last year didn't wreck this for them.

That day still haunts me and I can never take it back, but I will spend the rest of my days making it up to my sister. I have a recurring dream of when Smallie and River kidnapped me from outside the hospital while Ave was recovering. The shrill sound of her screams as they drove off with me in the back of that van still haunt me, even when I'm awake…as does the last time I laid my eyes on Corey Cox.

He's the one who got away. Not that I stood a chance with him but now that I'm out, it's time to focus on me. Love will come when I least expect it.

Flynn and Ave walk back inside and the smile on my sister's face is the biggest I've ever seen, she's beaming. I don't think I've ever seen her so happy. Cress races over and hugs Ave and then grabs her hand to get a look at the rock on her finger. Flynn and Preston do the man hug thing and they both then join us. Preston embraces Ave, after a nudging from Cress

"So how long have you two been banging?" I ask Cress, just as she takes a sip of the celebratory champagne. She spits it everywhere and her eyes widen in surprise but before she can answer, Lexi comes racing over.

"Mommy, I need to go poo poo," she says, crossing her legs and rocking on the spot.

Quicker than I have ever seen someone move in regard to shit, Cress jumps up, grabs Lexi's hand, and escorts her down the hallway to the bathroom.

"Saved by the poop," I say to Preston, who I notice hasn't said a word. He neither confirmed nor denied my question and in my experience, when people are silent, they are trying to come up with a rebuttal.

"Bay," Ave says, "leave her alone. It's been a rough time for them—"

"Lexi is doing much better now," Preston interrupts. "Cress and I are watching her like a hawk. I won't miss anything like that again."

"Miss what?" I ask. I'm genuinely concerned 'cause Lexi is a kick-ass kid.

Ave looks to me. "I'll fill you in later." She turns back to Preston, who kinda looks like Channing Tatum. "Glad all is well."

Cress returns with Lexi, who now has a lollipop and my mouth waters. I haven't had candy in so long. My mind drifts to Laffy Taffy and as if she's a mind reader, Ave walks over to me with a rectangular box and a smile breaks out on my face. "Is that what I think it is?"

"It might be."

"You are the best sister, ever," I tell her, grabbing the box and ripping it open. Two-point-five seconds later, I'm popping a purple chewy candy into my mouth. I close my eyes and savor the flavor, as a moan breaks free.

"Would you like us to leave you and your candy alone?" Ave says.

Opening my eyes, I look up and see everyone is staring at me. "It's sooo good."

"That purple shit is nasty," Flynn says, "I much prefer the green ones."

"Nah uh, buddy. Purple all the way."

We all head outside to enjoy the rest of the evening. We drink champagne and eat our weight in hors d'oeuvres; the food is amazing. It sure beats prison food, I'm going to end up so fat from eating all the things I missed out on while being locked up.

Looking around, I smile. Flynn outdid himself. The patio has been transformed into a romantic oasis. There's no way Ave would say no. It's such a romantic scene, and my mind drifts to Corey Cox. I wonder what the straitlaced sexy asshole is up to right now. I'm brought back to the present when Cress, Preston, and Lexi announce they are leaving. They say their goodbyes and soon after, it's just Flynn, Ave, and me.

Tonight could not have been more perfect, even Cress wasn't as annoying as I used to find her to be. Seems getting laid has mellowed the bitch. My sister is still beaming, Flynn went all out with the proposal but Ave deserves that and so much more. It's funny, the old me would have been majorly pissed off that my release from the slammer was overshadowed by the proposal, but seeing the happiness on my twinsie's face warms my little dead black heart.

Deciding I need some air, I excuse myself and head downstairs. Exiting the elevator, I pause mid-step when I see *him* standing in the lobby. My heart stops beating, I'm shocked at seeing him here. After that day, I never thought I'd see him again. Over the last twelve months he has gotten sexier, if that's possible.

He stops in front of me and we stare at one another. The air around us simmers and raises the temperature in the lobby. He speaks first and the sound of his voice vibrates through my body. Every nerve ending sparks to life and my clit jumps and pulses like it's at a rave. Twelve months of no contact and two words almost bring me to my knees.

I'm so screwed.

CHAPTER 22

Corey

"HELLO, KITTEN."

"I'm not your fucking Kitten," she spits at me. My eyes rake over her body and she's just as sexy as I remember.

"For a woman, you have such a potty mouth." My gaze drops to her lips and I remember the feel of them pressed against mine. Wrapped around my cock. Even though that occurred over twelve months ago, my body remembers as if it happened just moments ago.

"Fuck you, asshole. I'm not your Kitten. Never was and never will be."

"Kit—"

"You better watch your back, Cox. I have claws and I won't hesitate to use them on you. Now, what the fuck are you doing here? I've done my time. I'm a good girl now."

"I have no doubt you would scratch and mark me, but, Kitten," stepping into her personal space, I lean closer and whisper, "I promise you when it happens, you will be purring. All. Night. Long." Stepping back, I notice her swallowing deeply. *Score one for me* I think to myself. "I need to talk to you."

"What do you think we're doing now?"

"Don't sass me, Kitten." I see she's still sassy...and sexy as ever. "Can we go upstairs and talk? I have something important to discuss with you."

She shakes her head. "No, you can tell me here."

Looking around the lobby, it's empty except for the concierge and us. Stepping closer to her, I lower my voice. "Kye Vlahos escaped from custody today and a threat was made against me...and you."

She wobbles on her feet as my words sink in, "Wwww... what?" she says, her voice wavering. Any and all sass gone. "How?"

"He faked illness and managed to escape while in hospital."

"Why would he threaten me? He doesn't know I was a part of it, does he?"

"It looks like he knows. I think Creed Dawson told him."

"Fucking asshole, I'll kill him if I ever see him."

"That might be hard, he was murdered earlier today."

"What?"

I tell her about Creed's untimely death earlier today and mention the note threatening us. "I...I...we, I nee—"

"Kitten, listen to me." She lifts her gaze to mine and fear is etched all over her face. "I won't let anything happen to you. I have a man stationed out front and you will be protected." Stepping closer to her, I cup her cheek. "I promise." I run my thumb over her bottom lip. Her eyes droop closed. When she opens them, they are cloudy with desire. My head begins to lower to hers, but the moment is interrupted when I hear a soft voice from behind me. "Agent Cox, what are you doing here?"

Pulling away from Baylor, I turn to face her sister but before I can say anything, her eyes lock on Baylor and she immediately knows something is wrong. "BayBay, what's wrong?"

Baylor looks to her sister and hearing her voice unravels her. The floodgates open and she begins to cry. "Avie," she blubbers, falling to her knees. Covering her face with her hands, she cries as her sister embraces her in a sisterly hug.

The elevator doors open and my head snaps up, I see a gentleman step out, he looks familiar but I can't place him. His eyes lock with mine, then they drop to the sisters embracing and he races over to them. Squatting down, he rests his hand lovingly on Avery's back. "Ave, baby, what's wrong?"

She lifts her head to look at him. Concern is plastered all over her face. "I don't know," she tells him. "I came down to find Bay with Agent Cox and when she saw me, she fell apart."

"He's going to kill me," Bay murmurs.

"Who's going to kill you?" Ave asks her sister.

"Kye," she whispers.

"Who's Kye?" the man questions them.

"The guy Bay helped Agent Cox bring down. But he's in jail. I don't know what's going on." Avery stands up and turns to face me. "Care to explain, Agent Cox?" The tone of her voice reminds me so much of Baylor when she's pissed off.

"How about we take this upstairs?" Flynn says, looking over his shoulder toward the front desk. "We can discuss this in private."

"Good idea, Flynn." She looks to her sister. "Come on, Bay, let's get you upstairs."

Bay nods, but when she stands up, she wobbles on her feet and stumbles. Stepping forward, I wrap my arms around her. "I've got you, Kitten," I tell her, as I lift her up bridal style.

She wraps her arms around my neck and snuggles into my chest. As we walk toward the elevators, she whispers, "He's going to kill me," over and over again.

Following behind Avery and Flynn, I whisper, 'Shhhh' over and over, but she's lost in her mind right now. This isn't how I expected her to react. I was expecting my feisty kitten to tell me he can try, but no one will bring her down. I certainly didn't expect her to break down like this. I guess prison has mellowed her. My inner voice says, 'If you'd kept an eye on her, you'd know her better.' So many times over the last twelve months, I wanted to reach out. Make sure she was okay but the agent in me knew that was crossing a line.

The elevator doors open and we step into a gorgeous foyer. Flynn and Avery live in the penthouse, the four of us enter and my eyes dart around the place. Must be nice to have cash to spend on a flashy home like this. It's open plan with light walls, a large dark sofa with bright throw pillows, and doors leading to an amazing outdoor area. The kitchen is gorgeous. With dark chocolate-brown granite with wooden cabinetry, it's the ultimate dream kitchen.

Everyone walks to the living room and takes a seat on the sofa. Bending down, I go to place Baylor next to her sister, but she's gripping me tightly and not letting go. Turning around, I sit next to Avery with Baylor still attached to me like a monkey.

"What's going on, Agent Cox?" Avery asks.

"I got word today that Kye escaped. I came to warn Baylor to be on the lookout."

"Why do I feel there's more?" she questions.

This woman misses nothing. "As well as Kye escaping, Creed Dawson was murdered this morning in his cell."

"Ohh my God," she gasps, covering her mouth. "Does Cress know?"

"I'm not sure, but when Mr. Dawson was discovered, there was a note left."

"What did it say?"

"'Rats like to squeal. You and that bitch are going down.'"

"Oh My God," she says again, covering her mouth as the enormity of this sinks in.

"Will Bay be safe?"

"I will not let anything happen to her."

"What about you?" Flynn asks.

"I'll be fine. My concern is Baylor. I never imagined this would happen, if I had thought it would, I never would have used her to bring him down."

Baylor's head snaps up. "You used me," she growls, pulling away from me, she stands, and glares down at me. "You used me to get him and once you got your man, you tossed me aside like a piece of trash. Hell, you didn't even say goodbye after it all went down. I did exactly as discussed, I cozied up to the fucker. I pretended to want him. To be his queen. To be by his side. I did everything. Then once you got him, I became a footnote in your report. You forgot all about me." She turns and stalks toward the windows. She stops and takes a deep breath then spins to face me again. She points at me angrily. "You used me," she says softly, "and now my life is in danger because I tried to do the right thing." Tears streak down her cheek. "This always happens to me. I try do right and it all blows up in my face." She wipes away her tears and locks her eyes on me. "If I die, Cox, I will fucking haunt you for the rest of your days."

She turns and storms down the hallway. Slamming a door in anger, the force causes the doors out here to rattle. "Well, that went well," I say to break the silence.

Turning to face me, Avery stares at me. "She's right, you know."

"How so?"

"She did all this for you and then you ghosted her. After the moments you shared, she thought you cared, but in reality, you just did what was needed to get what you wanted."

Shaking my head, I protest, "That's not true at all. I...it's... it's complicated."

"You need to tell her that. She feels used and betrayed, and I don't blame her." The room falls silent again. "I think you should leave, Agent Cox." Avery stands. "You better keep Bay safe because if even a hair on her head is harmed, well, let's just say, you don't want to see what I'm capable of. If you think Baylor can be bitchy, wait until you meet 'Angry Avery', she has nothing on Bay. Agent Cox, my sister means the world to me. Sure, she's done some unsavory things, but she's owned her mistakes and has made up for them. You need to keep her safe so she can have her second chance."

Standing, I face Avery. "I will keep her safe." Walking to the door, I look over my shoulder with my hand on the door handle. "And for what it's worth. I do care about her...more than I should."

Opening the door, I step into the foyer and walk over to the elevator. Pressing the call button, I wait and think about what just went down. I realize how badly I fucked up when it came to Baylor and me. This is my chance to show her I don't just think of her as an informant. Maybe I will get my chance with Baylor Evans after all.

CHAPTER 23

Baylor

CURLING into a ball on my bed, I hug my knees and let it all out. I cry like I do when Thomas J dies in *My Girl*. I should have known something like this would happen. I never get a free pass, no matter what I do. Shit always hits the fan. This was meant to be my redeeming moment but now, now my life is on the line because I tried to do the right thing.

A knock on my door startles me, but I don't want to talk to anyone right now so I ignore it. Through the door, I hear Ave. "I'm here when you want to talk, BayBay. I love you."

"I love you too," I quietly whisper.

Rolling to my back, I let out a deep sigh and stare at the ceiling. Hours pass by and the events of the evening continue to play over and over in my head. One minute I'm over the moon to be released. Then I'm on another high celebrating my twinsie's engagement. And then it all comes crashing down around me when Cox tells me Kye escaped and that my life has been threatened.

Fuck. My. Life.

Closing my eyes, the image of Cox when I stepped out of the elevator pops into mind in high definition, full color vision. He really is a sexy-as-sin man. As soon as my eyes landed on him, my breath hitched. My heart started racing like I'd run a marathon and I'm no runner, so it was freakin' fast. My skin is still tingling from being in his arms. If only it wasn't due to my life being on the line. If only he was here to sweep me off my feet and ravage me.

At the thought of him ravaging me, my clit begins to tingle and throb. Sliding my hand down my body, my nipples pebble as I brush past them. Flicking open the button on my jeans, I slip my hand in and under the material of my panties. My clit sparks to life as I slide the pad of my finger over the ring and down between my folds. I'm wet already. Cox has that effect on me. My finger easily slides inside and I quietly moan. Biting my lip to keep myself quiet, I continue to thrust my fingers in and out, grazing my clit as my hand slides by. Gripping my breast through my shirt, I explode around my fingers. Moaning his name as I ride out the pleasure coursing through me.

Removing my fingers, I stand, grab my things, and skip across the hall to the bathroom and have a shower. I change into my pj's and once back in my room, I slip back into bed. The orgasm doing nothing to ease the worries swirling around my mind.

The next morning, I walk into the living area to find Ave at the kitchen counter with a coffee cup in hand. "Morning," I say, as I climb onto the stool across from her.

"Morning," she replies, as she fills a mug for me and hands it over to me. "Sleep okay?"

"Ish," I reply. Wrapping my hands around the mug, my palms warm from the heat of the hot black yummy nectar inside. Bringing the mug to my lips, I take a sip. Closing my eyes, I savor the flavor, my taste buds dancing and zinging to life. The coffee in prison was horseshit so to finally drink something good—no amazing—I can't help but moan.

"Would you like me to leave you and your coffee alone?" Ave teases, as she takes a seat on the stool net to me.

"Ave, you have no idea how shit the coffee was in there. This right here is everything."

"What's everything?" Flynn asks.

"Coffee," Ave and I say in unison.

Flynn leans down and kisses Ave on the top of her head. She leans back into him and closes her eyes. The love radiating between them is enough to heat an entire city block. Grabbing my mug, I slink back to my room, leaving the two lovebirds alone.

Snuggling down in the armchair in my room, I grab my Kindle and devour *Benched* by *Rebecca Barber*. I'm not normally a fan of the man bun but the way Rebecca describes Hunter-Caveman-Mitchell, I have been swayed.

A knock on the door pulls me away from my book and I smile when I see Ave. Her cheeks are flushed, indicating she and Flynn just got down and dirty. "Hey, what's up?"

"Just checking to see how you are? You disappeared earlier."

"I'm getting there. Yesterday was a lot, but I think I'm okay."

"You know you can talk to me."

Nodding, I place my Kindle down. "I know. I just don't want to rain on your parade. You should be celebrating your engagement. Not worrying if my mafia kingpin ex-boyfriend is going to make good on his promise."

"Well, I wasn't really worried about it until you put it like that. I was more checking on how you feel after being out? From all that I've read, it can be an adjustment for those being released."

A laugh escapes me. "Why am I not surprised that you looked all of this up?"

"What can I say, I like to know what to expect."

"Ave, I'm fine." I stand and walk over to her. "I promise."

"Just promise me you'll talk to me if things get too much?"

"Yes, Mom, I'll do that. Now, I'm going to walk to the store, get myself some wine and cheese, and then I'm going to binge watch movies all afternoon."

"Want some company?"

"I'd love some."

Ave and I do exactly that, Flynn even joins us. He just shakes his head when we watch *The Little Rascals* and recite every line word-for-word. The credits roll and I hop up to stretch, I've been sitting for too long. I look over to see Flynn and Ave making goo-goo eyes at one another. "Remember the first time we watched this together?" she asks him.

"How could I forget? You were naked and we ended up making sweet, sweet love 'til the wee hours of the morning," he not so quietly whispers.

"Lalalalalalalala," I singsong as I pop my fingers in my ears. "I don't need to hear this shit. That's one of those 'you know it happens but we don't talk about it' things."

They both laugh.

We tidy up the mess we made and we all head to bed. Just as I'm about to step into my room, Ave grabs my arm. "I'm taking you to brunch tomorrow." I try to interrupt her, but she commands, "Uh, don't argue. We're doing it."

"Yes, Mom," I tease again. "Night, guys."

In unison, they say, "Nite-nite," and head into their room.

Climbing into bed, I fall asleep immediately. The emotional toll of the last few days has finally caught up with me.

"This has been nice," I tell Ave, as I lift my mimosa and take a sip. The tang of the orange juice mixing with the tartness of the bubbles is the perfect combination…and it allows me to drink before midday, but then again, it's always 5:00 o'clock somewhere in the world.

"Yeah, it has. I can't remember the last time you and I brunched together," she says, as she shovels in a mouthful of her omelet.

"Probably before I went off the rails," I reply sadly, looking to the table.

Ave reaches over the table and squeezes my hand. "Bay, look at me." Lifting my gaze, I look at her. "That's in the past and it needs to stay there. Focus on the future and what's ahead."

"I'm trying but it's hard. With Kye on the loose, I'm pretty fucking scared, Avie," I honestly tell her. For the last two days, that's all I've thought about. I know that if he gets his hands on me, I'm dead. Literally.

"Cox won't let anything happen to you," she confidently says, but I'm not so sure. Kye is a crazy motherfucker, what I ever saw in him confuses me now. He's nothing like *him* but no one is like him. He's like the ultimate alpha that got away. And that there is another fucking problem in my life.

When I saw him two days ago, I was feeling all the emotions; angry at him for not saying goodbye or reaching out. He knew where I was, it's not like I disappeared, and then there's that attraction, which isn't just one-sided. I know he feels it too. The air definitely crackles when we are together. I haven't been with anyone since him. I think of that afternoon constantly and we never even had sex.

"He was that good, huh?" Ave asks me, as she takes a sip of her drink.

Nodding my head, my mind drifts to the feel of his tongue licking me. His fingers gripping my hips. Oh fuck, I need to get laid. "I need to use the bathroom."

Excusing myself, I stand up and walk toward the restrooms when I hear my name being screeched like a banshee. Turning around, I see Dr. Bitch aka Monica, Kye's side-piece standing next to Ave. Before I can say anything, she raises her hand and slaps Ave, hard across the face.

"You fucking bitch," she snarls, "I told Kye you couldn't be trusted and it looks like I was right."

"Oi, Monica, get your fucking hands off my sister."

Her head snaps to me and I storm toward them. "You okay, Ave?"

"I'm fine but I'm bloody sick of getting slapped in the face when it comes to Kye." My face scrunches in confusion. "I'll tell you later," she says, cupping her cheek.

Looking back to Monica, I stare at her. "What the fuck do you want?"

"I want to fucking kill you for what you did, you bitch. Kye doesn't deserve what you did to him."

"What I did?" I growl, "What I did? You do realize he is the worst of the fucking worst, right? You standing by his side shows you are just as bad as him. I'm not perfect, I know that better than anyone, but you two are the fucking scum between my toes." Ave giggles at my *The Little Rascals* reference. "I suggest you turn around and leave before I really show you how bitchy I can be."

"Watch your back, bitch," she snarls and then turns on her heel and storms out of the restaurant.

"You okay?" Ave asks me, resting her hand on my back in the reassuring way she does.

"Yes. No. I don't know," I tell her, the joy I felt not five minutes ago has vanished.

"Let's go home," she suggests.

Shaking my head at her, "No, let's enjoy our brunch. I'm not letting my salmon bagel or my mimosa go to waste."

Without a word, Ave sits down and lifts her drink. "A toast."

Lifting mine, I ask, "What are we toasting to?"

"To us, the Evans twins. Back together and better than ever."

"I'll drink to that."

Bringing my drink to my lips, the hairs on the back of my neck prickle. Looking over my shoulder, my mouth drops open and my breath hitches in my throat when I meet the evil stare of Kye Vlahos. But as quickly as I saw him, he's gone again. Clearly my mind is playing tricks on me again. I guess this situation is messing with my mind. Turning back to Ave, I focus on her. She's staring at the bling adorning her ring finger.

"I haven't seen you smile like that in a long time," I tell her.

She looks up at me, and she's beaming, her smile brighter than ever. "I'm happier than I've ever been, Bay. I have my sister back and I'm engaged to the most amazing man. Life is brilliant right now."

"I'm so so happy for you, Avie." Reaching across the table, I squeeze her hand.

We finish our brunch with no more interruptions or bitch-slaps. We decide to leave the car with the valet and head into the mall for a girls' day. We get manis and pedis. I spoil myself with a new pair of kick-ass purple heels and some lingerie. Lots and lots of purple lacy sexy lingerie. After wearing tighty whities for the last twelve months, I deserve a splurge.

We stop at Olive Garden and grab takeout for dinner. We have enough to feed an army but leftovers are always good. With our food in hand, we wait for the valet to bring Ave's car around. Staring up at the sky, I smile, it's a gorgeous sunset this evening. I missed views like this while being locked up.

"Gorgeous sunset, tonight," Ave says as I pop a taffy into my mouth. Before I can reply, all hell breaks loose.

CHAPTER 24

Corey

IT'S BEEN a few days since the proverbial shit hit the fan and every waking moment has me thinking about *her*, Baylor Evans. She has been at the forefront of my mind when I'm both awake and asleep. I think of her first thing in the morning. She's my last thought at night. I even dream about her. I've whacked off to visions of her, more in the last few days than I've whacked off in the last twelve months. I feel like I'm a horny teenage boy again,

Letting out a frustrated sigh, I lean back in my chair and close my eyes. Once again, the blonde-haired angel appears before me. A knock at my door has me sitting up in my seat and my happy thoughts disappear when I see Dean Chikatilo standing there.

"Hey, what's up?"

"Charli and I are heading to Bin 501, wanna join us?"

"Didn't pick you as a wine dude."

"I lost a bet so it was her choice."

"That's my girl," I tease, and the look he gives me is murderous. I really hate this asshole. "Sure, I'll meet you guys there in an hour."

"I'll let Charli know. See you soon," he says with a smile but it's sinister.

How Charli can work so closely with him amazes me, but then again, Charli is a tough badass who can deal with the best and worst of people. Hence, why she's great as a WitSec handler. The people she deals with are always colorful, with different backgrounds and varying levels of danger. She and Bay would definitely get along; thankfully those two won't ever be in the same room together.

Deciding to call it a day, I shut down my computer, grab my things, and head to my car to drive over to the bar to meet Charli and Dean. Traffic is light and I make it to there in record time. Looking to the sky, it's a vivid red and orange sunset this evening—it's absolutely gorgeous.

Opening the door, I step inside and immediately spot Charli and Dean. They look cozy together and a prickly feeling develops as I watch the two of them. Charli and I are friends, platonic friends, but seeing her with Dean right now doesn't sit right with me.

Making my way over to them, Dean looks up and a shocked expression appears on his face but he quickly schools it. "You made it," he says, his voice laced with shock.

"Yep, decided to cut out early."

"You sick, Cox?" Charli teases, "You never leave early."

"Trying something new." I shrug my shoulders and tell her, "You guys need a drink?"

They both raise their glasses. Nodding, I turn and head to the bar. There's an attractive brunette behind the bar. Her blue eyes are amazing, "What can I get ya?" she asks as I walk up to her.

"A glass of merlot, please."

"Coming right up." She spins on her heel and gets to preparing my drink. A guy walks up to her and places his hand on her lower back, he leans in, and whispers something to her. "Branson," she scoffs and hits him in the chest, "down, boy."

Clearly the two of them are together, the love radiating between the two of them is off the charts.

She replaces the cork in the bottle and walks back over to me. Placing the glass on the bar top. "Sorry, it's fuller than usual, but I got distracted." Her cheeks darken and the pink tinge is adorable on her face. Reminds me of a sassy blonde I know who rocks that shade when she's aroused. Dammit, I'm thinking of her again.

"No complaints here," I tell her, as I grab my wallet from my back jeans pocket but before I can pay, there's an explosion from outside, shaking the bottles and glasses behind the bar from its force.

Turning on my heel, I race toward the entrance and meet Charli and Dean. We step outside and my mouth drops open at the scene. "Fuck me," I growl, linking my fingers and resting my hands on the back of my head.

Shaking my head, I assess the scene before me and then I notice that the center of the blast came from where I parked. "My car."

"You were the target?" Charli asks, just as a hail of bullets start flying.

"Get down," I shout, as I throw myself at Charli, shielding her with my body.

A piercing pain shoots through my shoulder as Charli and I fall to the pavement. The wind is knocked out me, as the shock of being shot causes me to land not so gracefully.

Rolling off Charli, I stare at the gorgeous sky above. It's the last thing I see before darkness engulfs me in the blood red of the sunset sky.

An incessant beeping from beside me grates through my head. My eyes open and droop closed again. My eyelids feel like lead weights. Blinking repeatedly, I finally manage to keep them open. The room comes into focus and I realize I'm in a hospital bed. Then the events of the evening come crashing back to me.

Sitting up, I wince at the pull in my shoulder. Looking down, I see I'm shirtless and there's a bandage covering the bullet wound. I try to look behind me and see if it went through, but when I twist, a burning pain shoots through me.

"It was through and through," Charli says from next to me, I hadn't even realized she was here.

"Are you okay?" I ask, my eyes scanning her for injuries but she seems okay.

"Apart from a few bruises from having your lard ass crash-tackle me, I'm good." She pauses. "Thank you, Cox."

"Why are you thanking me?"

"I would have taken that bullet if you hadn't thrown yourself at me. So, thank you. I owe you one."

"You can repay me by getting me the fuck out of here. I hate hospitals."

"That I can do, but I don't think you'll like what I have to say next."

Before she can tell me the next batch of bad news, the door to my room opens and in walks Flynn Kelly, Baylor's sister's fiancé. "Corey, nice to see you awake."

"Nice to be awake." He steps into the room and I notice Charli slip out before the door closes. "So when can I get out of here, Doc?"

"You were just shot."

"But I didn't die."

He ignores me and continues, "The bullet went through so you didn't require surgery. It missed everything major, X-rays show no further damage but you will be sore for a few weeks. Try to rest up and keep the wound dry."

"So, sponge baths for the foreseeable future?" I raise my eyebrows at him.

"Sorry, I'm taken and bat for the other team," he teases, "but I will see what I can arrange on your behalf."

"Thanks, Doc, appreciate it." He nods and exits the room. A few moments later, Charli walks back in.

"All good?"

"As well as a gunshot can be, I guess." She still has that sheepish look on her face. "Out with it, woman. Whatever you have to tell me can't be any worse than my car getting blown up or being shot." She purses and lips and that's when I realize what she needs to tell me is worse than that. "Just tell me, Davis."

"An attempt was made on Baylor Evans' life at the same time as you were to be blown up. It's looking like it was a coordinated attack."

"Is she okay?" I ask, trying to sit up, but the pain in my shoulder is making the task difficult. Charli assists me into a sitting position.

"She's fine but the valet that she and Avery Evans were with, while they waited for their car, wasn't so lucky."

"Fuck me." I say, lifting my good arm to run over my face. "Where is she now?"

"Awaiting transfer to a safe house."

"That's good." I nod and look over at her and again, I can tell she's still hiding something. "What else is there?"

"You're going to the safe house with her," she says this really fast because she knows there's no way in hell I'm going into WitSec.

"Like fuck I am. I need to get out of here and bring down this motherfucker."

"Not happening, cowboy. Dean and I have been assigned to watch over the two of you up at Silver Springs Lake until he is back in custody."

"Like fuck you are," I scoff at her.

"Yes, fuck we are. You and Baylor Evans are officially in WitSec until Kye Vlahos is apprehended."

Flopping back to the bed, I shake my head in defeat and wince at the pain in my shoulder. I wanted to see her again; I didn't want to be living with her. Then I laugh, Baylor will *not* be happy with this. The next few weeks and/or months are going to be fun, seems I have three new roommates and one of them is my feisty little Kitten.

CHAPTER 25

Baylor

IT'S amazing how one minute you're staring up at the gorgeous sunset and the next, you're ducking for cover as bullets fly everywhere. Once again, Ave was in danger... because of me. We were both taken to the hospital to be checked out. Apart from a few scratches and bruises, we are fine. We were lucky, very lucky but the valet dude, not so much.

Flynn meets us in the ER and the scene between him and Avie was right out of one of the DL Gallie's romance novels I've been reading. It was perfect and romantic in every way, if you remove the ER, the attempt on our lives, and the disheveled state of both of us.

Flynn being Flynn, commands responsibility of our care. We are escorted into a treatment room and assessed immediately. We are waiting in the room when a lady walks in, reminding me of Lara Croft from *Tomb Raider*, which means she's kick-ass. I already like her and she hasn't even spoken a word.

"Baylor and Avery." She looks between us, unsure as to who is who.

"I'm Baylor," I tell her. "That's Ave," I add, flicking my thumb to Ave.

"Nice to meet you both. I'm Agent Charli Davis from WitSec. I've been assigned to watch over you, Baylor." She walks farther into the room and I take her in. Slim but muscular, with long dark chocolate-brown hair. Along with the Lara Croft vibe, she also reminds me of that chick from *One Tree Hill*, Sophia someone. She's badass and hot, basically she's the brunette version of me.

"Watch over me, how?" As soon as I say those words, I know that whatever comes next is going to suck major donkey balls.

"Due to the attempt made on your life today, you will be entering witness protection under my watch until Kye Vlahos is apprehended."

"Like fuck I am," I snap at her, she doesn't deserve my rage but it seems, once again, Kye is fucking with my life.

"I'm sorry, ma'am, you don't have a choice."

"Don't fucking call me ma'am."

"Baylor, language," Ave scolds me. "Look, I only just got you back but I agree with the agent. You need to go with her. I want you safe until this man is caught. I can't lose you, BayBay." She begins to cry and seeing her upset, upsets me, and my eyes well with tears too. "I won't lose you."

Wrapping my arms around her shoulders, I pull her in for a hug. "What about you?"

She pulls back and stares at me. "I have Flynn, he won't let anything happen to me. I'll be safe."

"And we will have someone watching her since you look so alike," the agent adds. "Avery, you need to remain vigilant in the coming weeks."

"I will, I promise. Just keep my BayBay safe."

"Is there any other way?" I plead. "Can I speak with Corey Cox? He was my original handler person."

"He, umm, ahh, is unavailable right now." Her response is confusing to me.

Taking a deep breath, I purse my lips. I really want to flip her off and run away but the new me relents, "Then I guess, I'm going with you." It's hard, and no fun, being good.

"Glad you are coming willingly, Baylor. I'll give you a few moments to say goodbye to your sister, and I'll arrange for my partner to escort you there. I'll join you later once I've finalized a few things here in the city." Again I get the feeling she's hiding something from me but before I can press her, she exits the room leaving Ave and I alone.

Looking back to my sister, I see tears in her eyes. "Don't cry, Avie, I'll be fine."

"But I just got you back."

"And I'll be back again soon...ish."

"But what if—"

"Nope, no what-ifs. I will be back. Promise."

She wraps her arms around me, tighter this time. I do the same. We hug each other, squeezing each other for dear life. A knock on the door pulls us apart, we look over and in steps Flynn with a guy I recognize from the day the bust went down. He gives me the heebie-jeebies.

"I'm Dean Chikatilo, I'll be your escort today."

"I'm Baylor. This is my twinsie, Ave, and her fiancé, Flynn."

"Nice to meet you all. Ms. Evans, we must get moving. Say your goodbyes and leave your phone and purse with your sister."

"I can't take anything with me?"

"I'm afraid not. Everything you need will be provided."

"Ohh, okay then." Standing, I look at Ave. "I guess this is goodbye, again."

She shakes her head. "No! It's not goodbye, it's I'll see you later."

"See you later, I like that." We hug each other one last time and surprisingly, Flynn wraps his arms around the two of us. Ave and I are both blubbering when I pull away.

"I love you, BayBay," she tearfully says.

"Love you too, Avie."

Turning away from my sister, I follow Agent Chikatilo out of the room. The sound of Ave crying stays with me as we walk away.

He escorts me to an awaiting van, opens the door, and I climb in. He follows and takes the seat next to me. Looking to the front seat, I see Agents Hall and Oats. "What's up, guys?" I say.

"Ms. Evans," they both say in their stick up their ass, hoity-toity agent way. Turning back to face the front, they pull away from the hospital curb. Settling in, my eyes become heavy and I drift off to sleep.

I'm shaken awake. "We're here," Agent Chikatilo says, before he opens his door and hops out. He comes around to my side, opens my door, and offers me his hand. I take it and he helps me out. My body is stiff from the uncomfortable position I was in, we drove through the night and the sun is just starting to rise.

Behind the gorgeous cabin is a lake. "Where are we, Agent Chikatilo?"

"Silver Springs Lake," he tells me, as we begin walking toward my new home. "And call me Dean. We'll be together for the foreseeable future and my full name is a mouthful and a half. So Dean is fine."

Nodding my head, a creepy feeling runs over me. I don't like this guy but since we will be roomies for who knows how long, I smile at him before turning my attention to the cabin before me, it's gorgeous. This won't be such a bad place to live for the foreseeable future. It has a rustic charm to it with a wraparound porch, shutters, and planter boxes. Climbing up the few stairs, we walk around the side and my mouth drops open at the view before me. The cabin sits right on the lake and has its own private jetty. Looking around, there doesn't seem to be any other dwellings nearby, hence why we are here, dear Baylor.

Dean unlocks the door and steps to the side to let me pass. Stepping inside, I find I'm in the kitchen. This place is nothing like I pictured. I imagined a dingy room in the bumfuck of nowhere. I got the bumfuck part right but the living quarters, I was way off base. Looking around, I smile at the room before me. It's a dreamy country-inspired kitchen; I'd love to bake up a storm with Avie in here. The farm-style sink sits under a picturesque window that overlooks the outdoor patio area and lake. An island counter with a marble top sits in the middle. The rich wooden cupboards complement the hardwood floors. Past the kitchen is the dining room and off that a large living room with stone fireplace. Off the living room is a hallway leading to the bedrooms, bathroom, and stairs up to the master suite.

"Dibs on master suite." I shout, as I make my way over to the stairs.

"No, can do," Dean retorts, stopping me in my track as I step onto the first step. "You need to be on the ground floor so we can easily protect you."

"Fuck that," I snark, as I make my way up the stairs and much to my dismay, there are already things in that room. Turning around, I stomp back downstairs.

"Who's up there?"

"Charli," he says, as he walks past me and heads down the hallway. "This is yours," he says, stopping in front on the first door. "Mine is down the hall across from the laundry and next to the bathroom."

Nodding, I walk into my room and sit on the bed. *At least the mattress is comfy*, I think as I flop back.

"Get some sleep," he tells me, "Charli will be here in a few hours and then we can go over everything."

Nodding, I stay where I am and I drift off to sleep straightaway.

I'm woken a few hours later from an amazing dream. As I wake up, I must still be in my dreamland because I hear *his* voice, as if he's here with me. Shaking my head, I wipe the sleep from my eyes. Swinging my legs over the edge, I sit there for a few moments and when I hear his voice again, I realize it wasn't a dream. He IS here.

Standing up, I walk down the hallway but before I make myself present, I stop and listen to them talking…about me.

"She's a wild one," Dean says.

"That's the understatement of the century but she's… she's, I have no words for Baylor Evans."

Hearing that pisses me off, so I make my presence known. Dean and Corey both turn their heads to look at me. Corey is sitting on the sofa and Dean is in the armchair. "And I have no words for you too, asshole," I snap. "I'm in this mess because you guys didn't do your job."

"Baylor—"

It's the first time he's used my real name in forever and hearing that hurts, he's always called me Kitten. Clearly, I mean nothing to him. My anger and hurt explode and I scream at him, "I fucking hate you!"

"I fucking hate you, too!" he spits back at me. "You're a stuck-up, pain in my ass who won't take responsibility for anything. It's always someone else's fault."

"For once, asshole, this isn't my fault. Creed fucking Dawson ratted on me and now I'm stuck here in the bumfuck of nowhere with you, Lara Croft, and Agent Wankstain." He has to hide the laugh right now. "What the fuck are you laughing at?"

"Watch your mouth, Kitten."

"You're not the boss of me."

"No, I am," Lara Croft aka Agent Davis says, as she steps into the living room from the kitchen. "I suggest the two of you learn to live together because for the foreseeable future, we will all be living in close quarters." She emphasizes the word all.

"As long as HE stays out of my way, I have no problem."

"As long as SHE stays out of my way, I have no problem."

Corey and I stare intently at one another, these next few months are going to be fun...or not.

CHAPTER 26
Corey

BAYLOR and I continue to glare at one another. It's a Mexican standoff and neither one of us is willing to make the first move and concede defeat. This woman is frustratingly stubborn but guess what, Kitten? So am I.

Dean stands up and breaks the silence, "I'm doing a perimeter check." He heads toward the front door and exits the cabin.

"Great," Charli says, "I'll get started on lunch." She turns around and walks back the way she came.

Now it's just Baylor and me in the living room. We continue to stare at one another. Surprising me, she walks over and sits down next to me. That's when she notices my shirt undone and the bandage covering me.

"What happened?" she questions, and I hear genuine sincerity in her tone.

"Got shot," I tell her.

"Kye?" she questions.

"Courtesy of him, yes."

"Are you okay?"

"Yeah," I reply nodding my head. "Takes more than a car bomb and a few bullets to bring me down."

Her eyes widen at my confession. I see concern in her eyes and I hate that she's hurting for me. I hate that this is all because I brought her in. I never should have floated this idea because now, she's in WitSec and that asshole is roaming free.

"Baylor," I say, while at the same time she says, "Corey."

We both laugh. "You first," she says.

"I'm sorry," I tell her.

She scrunches her face in confusion and it's adorable to see. "Why are you sorry?"

"You're in this mess because of me."

She shakes her head from side to side. "No, I'm in this mess because of me and a fucking psycho, narcissistic, dickwad asshole named Kye Vlahos."

"Watch your mouth, Kitten." She smiles when I say this. "Why are you smiling?"

"You called me Kitten again."

"I always call you Kitten."

She shakes her head, "Not since arriving here. You've called me Baylor and while I like the way you wrap your tongue around my name, I prefer when you call me

Kitten." She purses her lips. "It's almost as if you care." She lifts her head and stares at me.

"Kit—" but before I can answer her, Charli pops her head in.

"Lunch is ready."

Baylor smiles at me and hops up, offering me her hand when she notices I'm struggling to stand on my own. Placing my palm in hers, an electrical current zaps between us. From the look on her face, she felt it too. She pulls me into a standing position and we stare at one another. Her blue eyes are so radiant in the light; it feels like she's staring deep into my soul. "

"Thank you," I tell her, that's when she realizes she's still holding my hand. She quickly drops it and steps around me toward the dining room. She looks over her shoulder and states, "I'm glad he didn't kill you." Then she turns around and continues on.

Shaking my head, I follow, and when I enter, my eyes widen at the spread before me. "Holy shit, Charli, when did you become a MasterChef? This all looks amazing."

"It's nothing," she nonchalantly says as she takes a seat next to Baylor.

Taking my seat across from Baylor, my eyes take in all the food before us. There's two different salads, chicken strips, chicken skewers, dinner rolls, corn on the cob, and behind her on the counter are her famous brownies. "Can I just skip to dessert?"

"Not until you eat your salad," she tells me.

"Yes, Mom," I tease.

She flips me the bird. "Just sit down, asshole."

"How come you don't get mad at her for swearing?" Baylor asks me as she fills up her plate.

"She owns a gun and knows how to use it," I tell her, placing a chicken skewer on my plate.

Baylor looks to Charli. "Think you can teach me to shoot?"

Charli nods. "Sure."

As I growl, "No fucking way."

"Watch your mouth," the two of them sass me in unison.

"Jinx!" Baylor yells at Charli.

"Double jinx!" Charli shouts back.

"Triple jinx." Baylor's throws back at her with a laugh.

"Quadruple jinx," Charli sasses in return, leaving Baylor speechless. And then the two of them cackle like hyenas. Putting these two together is going to be trouble; I can just see it now.

"Oh My God, it's like dealing with children," I say, biting into a chicken skewer.

"Your just jealous you didn't get to play," Charli says, taking a sip of her soda.

"Yeah, so jealous," I sarcastically reply.

"Why you jealous?" Dean asks, the kitchen door slamming shut behind him. He sits next to me, fills a plate, and digs in.

"Wash your hands, you grub," Baylor says, her face scrunched up.

"Fine," he huffs, standing up he walks into the kitchen and washes his hands.

"So how do you two know each other?" Baylor asks Charli.

"Corey and I went through the academy together and over the years we've stayed in touch. Met here and there on cases. This is a first though."

"How so?"

"He's the first colleague I've had under my protection. It's a little daunting, to be honest."

"Pffft," I tell her, "there's nothing daunting about me."

"I agree," Dean says, rejoining us. "Just like you, Baylor, he's just another witness we're babysitting. He's nothing special." He looks to me. "No offense."

"None taken," I tell him, but from the tone of his voice, I know he's full of shit. This guy really grates on my nerves, it was easy to mask it when I'd only see him here and there but living with him, well this is going to be fun.

Looking across the table, I see Charli and Bay chatting away. Those two clicked immediately. It's nice to see Bay finally relaxing. When I first saw her earlier and we began to fight, that wasn't how I wanted this to go. What I really want to do with her is not appropriate but ever since I saw her almost a week ago now, I've wanted nothing more than to fuck the life out of her.

Dean nudges me and asks, "You gonna tap that?"

"What?" I ask him, unsure if I heard him correctly.

"You gonna tap that?" he says, enunciating each word and royally pissing me off.

"Charli and I are friends. Nothing more," I tell him, but I know he's referring to Baylor. I know that what I want and what I should do are two different things and I really don't want to voice it aloud.

"Not referring to her."

Looking to him, I stare at him, unsure what to say.

"Your silence tells me everything." He stands up, leans down, and quietly whispers, "I'd tap it the first chance I got."

Grinding my molars, I glare at him and breathe deeply. It's taking every ounce of my strength to not deck this mother-fucker right now. If I hated him before, now I despise him.

He laughs as he grabs his empty plate and walks into the kitchen.

Watching him walk away, I feel her eyes on me. Turning my head, my gaze catches her and we stare at one another. She brushes a tendril of blonde hair behind her ear and smiles. It punches me right in the heart and it hits me. Ohh fuck, I'm falling for Baylor Evans.

CHAPTER 27

Baylor

...two weeks later

ONCE AGAIN, the sun is shining brightly but as soon as the sun starts to dip, there's a chill in the air. I'm sitting out on the end of the jetty with a coffee in hand and a bag of taffy. Someone, I'm guessing Corey, arranged for them to appear in the groceries each week.

Sitting out here, it's my happy place. It's so peaceful. When I sit out here, it's as if everything is right with the world. I pretend I'm not in WitSec. I pretend that Corey is my husband watching me from the deck of the house and not an agent also under protection. Charli is my best friend and not our handler. The best friend part is the only true statement. She and I bonded immediately, I feel as if I've known her longer than two weeks. The only thorn in my side is Dean. There's something about him that grinds me the wrong way, but I can't put my finger on it.

If it wasn't for Charli, I don't know that I'd be able to survive this. Charli really is a kick-ass chick and my original assessment of her being a cross between Lara Croft and that chick from *Chicago PD* is one-hundred-percent true. Her mannerisms remind me so much of Ave, she calms me in the way Ave does. Thinking of Ave, it hits me right in the chest how much I miss her. I miss her like crazy. At least when I was in prison we could talk on the phone, but while I'm here, it's radio silence. I'm not sure how much longer I can take the isolation. Being here is different from my time on the inside. In prison, I had jobs to keep me busy. But here, there's not much to do at all. Living with three people is hard, especially when one of those three is a douchecanoe, wankstain asshole.

The jetty jiggles and I know my serenity will be broken any minute, but I don't mind because I know it's *him* coming to join me. Whenever he's near, the air around me crackles and zings to life. I've never felt this before, but it can never be more than a fantasy. If our circumstances were different, I'd make a move but I know that once this is all over, he'll go back to being the sexy-assed agent he is, and me, well I have no clue what I'm going to do. I do know that Bitchy Baylor has left the building; I just wish I knew what I wanted to do with my life.

"It's beautiful out here," he says, taking a seat next to me.

"It sure is. Sitting here at the end of jetty is my most favorite spot to be."

"I guessed that."

"How so?" I ask.

"You're down here each and every day." I laugh. "You know, it's probably not the safest spot to hang out."

"There's no one around for miles. We are literally in the bumfuck of nowhere."

"You underestimate Kye. He will find us."

"You trying to scare me?"

"No," he says shaking his head. "Just being realistic. And I…" He drifts off.

Turning to face him, I rest my hand on his knee. "And I what?" I ask. I really want him to finish that sentence.

"I don't want to see you get hurt."

"Awww, does the big bad agent care about me?"

"Yes, I do," he honestly tells me. His eyes are locked intently on me. In this light, I can see flecks of gold around his irises. He really has the most mesmerizing eyes. "Kitten, I don't want anything to happen to you. You're here because I didn't protect you."

"Cox, no," I say, shaking my head. "I'm in this mess because Kye Vlahos is a fucking psychotic asshole, who thinks the world owes him. Now, before you berate me for my language, there are no other words to describe him so I'm given a pass when it comes to him."

He smirks and I find myself grinning back at him.

"You really are something," he tells me.

"Something good or something bad?"

"Something that could get me into a lot of trouble," he lifts his hand and brushes a strand of hair behind my ear, "but it would totally be worth it."

We both fall silent, processing the words he just uttered. My eyes drop to his lips and I want him to kiss me. It would be the most perfect moment, and we start to lean forward. We are millimeters away from kissing when the sound of an engine has Cox pulling away. Seconds later, Charli comes racing down.

"Inside, now!" She demands.

"Kitten, go," Cox says.

"You too, Cox."

He stands up and offers me his hand. He pulls me up and we flee toward the house. My heart is racing when we step inside the kitchen. Corey locks the door behind us and we walk to the windows and watch as Charli stands on the end of the jetty and talks to driver of the boat.

As I watch, my heart beats faster and faster. Fear rumbles through me. My breathing is labored and my vision begins to dot. I wobble on my feet but Cox catches me. "Breathe, Kitten."

Blinking rapidly, I feel like I'm going to pass out. Corey grips my cheeks and lifts my gaze up to him. "Focus on my voice, Kitten. Deep breaths. Slowly," he soothes. Gently, he runs his fingers along my cheekbone. "Breathe in. Breathe out." He mimics the breathing motion and somehow, my body follows his lead.

My breathing and vision return.

My heart rate begins to slow down.

My body and senses relax.

My skin prickles and comes back to life at his soothing touch.

Lifting my hands, I cover his on my cheeks. Looking into his eyes, I feel secure in his embrace and I know, he'd do anything to keep me safe.

Without thinking, I lift to my tippy-toes and press my lips to his. He doesn't kiss me back and I feel like I've made a mistake, but then it happens. His tongue pushes through my lips and into my mouth. He's kissing me back. It starts out slow but it quickly turns heated and carnal.

It's the best fucking kiss of my life.

Wrapping my arms around his neck, I pull him farther into me, deepening the kiss and our connection. You can't tell where he starts and I end. We become one as our tongues continue to slip and slide in and out of each other's mouths.

He spins us around and with our lips fused, he walks me backward through the living room, down the hall, and into my bedroom. Once across the threshold, he kicks the door closed and guides us toward the bed. The back of my knees hit the mattress, instead of pushing me down, he lifts me up, spins around, and sits on the edge of the bed with me straddling him.

His cock presses into me, I can feel every ridge because I'm only wearing black leggings sans panties. He grips the hem of my purple slouchy sweater and pulls it over my head. Our lips separate for a few moments but as soon as the material passes, our mouths are once again joined.

He slides his hand around my ribs and unclasps my bra. Slipping the straps down my arms, my skin comes alive at the brief touch of his fingers. Dropping it to the carpet, he kisses down my neck toward my breasts. My head drops back, pushing my chest toward him. He cups my boobs and sucks the taut peak into his mouth. "Fuuuuuuuuck," I moan at the sensation.

Lifting his gaze to mine, I stare into his heated eyes. I know he wants to berate me for swearing so, I taunt him, "Maybe you should spank me?" But the joke's on me, before I can process what's happening, I'm flying through the air and I land on my stomach on the bed. He grabs the top of my leggings and pulls them down, exposing my ass. He runs his hand gently over the cheek and my skin breaks out in goosebumps at his touch. They quickly disappear and they're replaced with a stinging sensation. The asshole slapped my ass.

"Did you just fucking slap my ass?"

"Yes," he growls, as he lands another two slaps in quick succession.

"Fuck," I cry out.

"Watch your mouth or I'll fill it with something to shut you up."

He slaps my ass again and again. My insides quiver and I moan in delight. "You like me slapping your sexy ass, Kitten?" he whispers into my ear, as he slaps me repeatedly. My desire building each time his hand connects with my flesh.

"Please," I beg, rubbing myself against the comforter but I can't quite reach where I need to be rubbed.

"What are you begging me for, Kitten?"

Looking at him over my shoulder, I tell him honestly, "Everything."

CHAPTER 28

Corey

THAT ONE WORD is music to my ears.

My cock was already hard but hearing her say that has it painfully pressing against the zipper of my cargos. Flicking open the button, I'm about to lower my fly when there's a knock at the door. "Living room, now," Dean yells out.

Baylor is staring at me, breathing heavily. "To be continued," I reassure her, bending down and pressing my lips to hers. She rolls onto her back and wraps her arms around my neck, pulling me down so I'm cocooning her. I give myself over to her and the kiss.

Nothing else matters right now except for Bay's breasts pressing into my chest and my tongue plunging in and out of her mouth. Another banging interrupts. "Now!" Dean roars. Clearly we lost ourselves in each other and lost track of time once again.

Staring down at her, I brush her hair off her forehead and cup her cheek. "Kitten, we WILL continue this later."

She nods her head and reluctantly, I climb off her. Standing up, I readjust my cock and redo the button. Outstretching my hand, I offer it to Baylor. She places her tiny hand in mine and I pull her into a sitting position. My eyes drop to her tits.

"My eyes are up here, buddy."

"I know," I tell her with a wink, "but have you seen your tits? I have no words."

"I see them every day. There's nothing special about them," she says, as she climbs off the bed and pulls her leggings back into place. She reaches down for her bra and unfortunately for me, she slips it back on. Bending down, I grab her sweater and hand it to her. "Thanks," she whispers, putting it back on. She's only wearing leggings and a sweater but fuck me sideways, she is a vision.

Another pounding on the door startles Bay and she jumps at the sound. "Coming," I shout, as I walk to the door and swing it open.

"Already?" Dean teases, "Thought you had more stamina than that, Cox."

"Fuck you, asshole," I spit at him. Pushing past him, I make my way down the hall.

"I don't know what you see in him when you could have me," I hear Dean say to Baylor, spinning around, I'm ready to let loose on him when Baylor steps into the hallway. She backs him up to the wall opposite her room, and she places her hand on his chest. "I don't know why you'd even think I'd want to be with you, but I'll spell it out for you. He has none of your characteristics. The possibilities with him are endless. He thinks of me as a person and just not a possession. Those are just a few of the things that make him, and not you, appealing to me." Tapping his cheek, she smiles and walks away. Just as she reaches Charli and me, she looks over her shoulder and adds, "And have you seen his ass?" She squeezes my ass for effect and continues down the hall.

Charli and I both laugh at her reply and follow her into the living room. She curls her legs under herself on the sofa and waits for us. Charli sits next to Bay, while I lean on the sofa arm next to her. She presses her head onto my thigh and I smile at the contact.

Dean finally joins us, and he looks pissed off but Charli doesn't give him a chance to whine like the little bitch he is. "Dean, take a seat, we need to talk," Charli says, breaking the silence.

Dean drops into the armchair. "What's up, boss lady?"

"That was a close call earlier. Baylor, I don't want you going down to the jetty anymore. That boat could have been Kye and his men. We can't take that risk."

"But—" she tries to interrupt.

"No buts. Your safety is my number one priority."

"Can I still go outside? Or am I trapped in here like an animal at the zoo?"

"Accompanied? Yes. Alone? No."

"I feel like I'm in prison again," she says.

"I'm sorry, Baylor, but I can't risk it." She looks to Dean. "I want you to recheck the perimeter."

"I did it this morning," he snaps back at her.

"I want you to do it again."

"Fine," he grunts. He stands and exits through the front door, slamming it behind him.

"What's his problem?" Baylor asks us.

"You just rejected him. He doesn't take too kindly to women doing that."

"Well, he shouldn't be such a douchehole."

I laugh at Baylor's assessment of Dean. "How do you put up with him as a partner?" I ask Charli.

"He never used to be like this but he's changed in the last few weeks. He's being secretive and his mind isn't on the job."

"Should I be worried?" Bay asks.

"No," Charli and I say together.

"Bay, I'm not going to let anything happen to you." I tell her, "You need to listen to Charli's orders. If you do that, you'll be safe."

"What about you guys?"

"We'll be fine. We're trained for this," Charli reassures her. "I need to call HQ and update them on our visitors today. Can I trust you to behave?"

We both nod our head. It appeases Charli because she heads upstairs to make her call.

I take a seat on the coffee table in front of Bay. "You okay?" She nods but I don't believe her. "I call bullshit."

"How can you be so calm about this?"

"It's my job to be calm. You just need to trust us and relax."

She stares at me and she bites her lip. "I think I know how we can relax." She shuffles to the edge of the sofa and stands up. She stretches out her hand to me. With a smile, I place mine in hers. Lacing our fingers together, she pulls me back down the hallway and into her room. She closes the door behind her and turns to face me.

"You, Agent Cox, have far too many clothes on."

"As do you, Ms. Evans."

"Call me Kitten," she seductively says, lifting her sweater over her head then dropping it to the floor.

"Okay, Kitten, you still have too many clothes on."

She grips the top of her leggings and ever so slowly peels them down her legs. She pulls them off and stands up. With her eyes locked on me, she reaches behind her back and removes her bra. She is gloriously naked before me.

Licking my lips, I step to her. I need to touch her. She grabs my hand and shakes her head. "Uhh ah, Agent Cox. You cannot touch me until you remove your clothes, too."

Quicker than I have ever stripped off before, I remove my shirt, cargos, and briefs. The discarded items join Baylor's clothes on the floor. "Much better," she purrs, as the little minx slides her finger down the valley between her breasts.

Mimicking her words from before, I reach out and grab her hand. "Uhh ah, Kitten. Your body is mine."

She lifts her gaze to mine. "Have at it then, Agent Cox."

CHAPTER 29

Baylor

STANDING NAKED BEFORE HIM, my heart beats faster than it ever has before. How I can be turned on right now, when not five minutes go, my safety was once again in jeopardy, is beyond me. But when it comes to Agent Corey Cox, my rational thinking takes a vacation.

He steps toward me like I'm his prey, sliding one hand around my waist and the other into my hair. He tugs me into him and slams his lips against mine in a heated all-consuming kiss. *I fucking love kissing him.* I feel his kiss all over my body. My skin is heated and thrumming with desire for the man before me.

"Please," I murmur against his lips.

He breaks the kiss. "What do you want me to do, Kitten?"

"Everything," I tell him, and it's true. I want him in every way possible. He may piss me off to no end but at the same time, he turns me on. He brings my body to life in a way I've never felt before.

"Everything it shall be, then." He smirks at me. Gripping my waist, he throws me over his shoulder and walks us over to the bed. Resting a knee on the mattress, he drops me down and I bounce a few times. A giggle breaks free.

"I love when you laugh like that," he tells me, his eyes eating me up.

"I love having you make me laugh like this." I stare up at him and take a moment to appreciate the fine specimen before me. Abs on abs. The elusive V pointing to his cock, his impressive cock. There isn't an ounce of fat on the man. He is muscular in the most delicious way. There are no tan lines on the man; he is hot AF.

"Like what you see?" he cockily says.

My eyes snap up to his. "Fuck yes, I do. I want to lick every crevice on your body. I want to suck your dick until you see stars. I want to kiss you forever, but most of all, I want—no I need—you to fuck me into next week, right this fucking second."

"Normally I'd tell you to watch your mouth, but fuck, Kitten, I want all of that too. You are a vision and we will not be leaving this room until I have explored every inch of your delectable body. Now get ready, 'cause, Kitten, I'm about to fuck you. All. Night. Long." He enunciates the last three words and my body, which was already buzzing with desire, quivers with what's about to happen.

"Have at it, Agent Cox." I lie back into the pillows and spread my legs wide. Sliding my hand down my body, I flick my clit ring before slipping my finger between my folds but before I can insert a finger, he grips my wrist.

"Uh ah, Kitten. That pussy is mine." Before I can protest, he lowers his head and licks me from taint to clit. He sucks on my piercing as he thrusts his fingers inside of me, and immediately I see stars. "Fuuuuck," I moan in delight, as he continues to assault me with his tongue and fingers. He hooks his finger around inside of me and I explode. I scream his name as the most intense orgasm of my life slams into me like a wave to the shore in the middle of a Category 5 hurricane.

My body is mush when he removes his fingers and face from between my thighs and stares down at me. "I love that shade on you."

"What shade?" I breathlessly ask him.

"Just fucked pink."

"Don't think I've seen that color at Sephora."

"You won't ever see it there because it's a limited edition color that's solely for me."

I don't know how to reply to him, so I lift my hand and beckon him to me with my finger. Like a panther stalking his prey, he crawls up my body. He doesn't touch me but his nearness is enough to have my body coming to life again. He hovers above me, staring deeply into my eyes. I see nothing but lust and desire reflecting back at me.

Reaching up, I cup his cheek. "Where have you been all my life?"

"Catching bad guys and waiting for you and your sassy mouth to be in interrogation three."

His words cause the smile on my face to drop, he's right. We met because I'm a criminal and he's an agent, but before I can dwell any further, he covers my hand with his. "Don't go there. Stay here with me. Think of the here, the now, and what's next."

"And what IS next?"

"Me fucking you."

"About fucking time."

"Kitten."

He growls my name in warning to my excessive swearing, but I love taunting him. I stare at him and smirk. "Fuck. Me. Now."

"You're asking for another spanking."

"I'm down with that but first—" I don't get to finish my taunt because he thrusts himself deep inside of me. I thought I saw stars when he used his fingers and tongue but fuck me sideways, I'm seeing the whole fucking universe right now.

He lowers his head and kisses me aggressively. His tongue thrusts in sync with his cock with perfect timing. Wrapping my arms around his neck, I hold on tightly as he fucks the life out of me.

"Coooooorey," I moan, as his cock continues to fill me up. He slides in and out, hitting that magical spot with each thrust.

"Come for me, Kitten," he demands against my lips. I want to tell him to go fuck himself, but it's like he knows my body because I'm right on the cusp. He slips his hand between us and when he presses on my piercing, it's just what I need. I scream his name as another intense orgasm unleashes.

My walls clench his cock and my juices soak the mattress below. His body tenses and he, too, comes, his seed spilling deep inside of me. My eyes widen when I realize we didn't use protection. Looking up at him, I see the recognition on his face too.

"Fuck," he spits.

"We just did," I say with a laugh, wanting to lighten the mood. Loosening my grip around his neck, I smile at him. "Don't worry. I'm clean and on the pill."

"I'm clean too. I've never been careless like that before but with you, all rational thoughts left my body. All I could focus on was sliding into you and fucking you."

My grin widens at his words. He climbs off the bed and walks to the door, he looks out, then darts across the hall to the bathroom. He returns with a washcloth. He kicks the door closed and proceeds to wipe me clean. I was worried that after we did the deed, it would be awkward but it's not. I'm happy and content. At that thought, my smile drops because lately, whenever I'm happy, shit soon hits the proverbial fan.

"What's wrong?" he asks me as he climbs back onto the bed, pulling me into his side. I snuggle in, throwing a leg over him, and running my fingertips over his chest.

"It's nothing."

"Don't lie to me, Kitten, what's got you frowning?"

"I'm happy," I honestly tell him.

"That's a good thing."

A laugh escapes me. "I know that but my with my track record, whenever I'm happy, it all turns to shit."

"That was then. This is now." He tells me and places a gentle, reassuring kiss on my temple. It instantly calms me —and it hits me—he calms my inner beast. He brings out the goodness I have buried deep down.

"How do you do that?" I ask him. Lifting my head off his chest, I rest my cheek in my palm and I look up at him.

"Do what?" His face is laced with confusion.

Sitting up, I spin around and cross my legs. I stare down at him and smile. "Put me at ease with your words. You calm me, Corey. Ave was the only one to ever do that but since I met you, you've brought me to life and make me look at things in a different light. You've dug deep inside of me and you're pulling out the best version of me."

"Kitten, I haven't done anything. That's all you. If I remember correctly, you told me to go fuck myself when I first offered you that deal. Sitting here now, I wish I had listened to you," my face drops at his words, "no, not like that." He sits up and faces me. We are both naked having a pretty deep conversation right now. "If you hadn't of agreed to go undercover, you'd be back in the city living a good life. Instead, you're trapped here because you helped me."

"And I'd do it again because it was the right thing to do."

"Your big heart is one of the many things I love about you." My eyes widen at the mention of love. Sure I have feelings for him, and he does for me, but love, no. No one will ever love me. "If anything, you've brought me to life. I now see life in color rather than just black and white."

"You really are something else, Corey Cox."

"As are you, Baylor Evans. Now come here, I need to fuck you again."

And that's what we do for the rest of the night. I lose count as to how many orgasms he pulls from me but I do know one thing, after last night, I have completely fallen for Agent Cox.

CHAPTER 30
Corey

WAKING THE NEXT MORNING, I smile when I realize it wasn't a dream. Baylor and I finally fucked and I can unequivocally say, it was the best night of my life. But what surprises me the most is my feelings for her have grown dramatically in the last twelve hours. She constantly surprises me. Sure, she puts up a bitchy front, but underneath all that is a woman with a beautiful soul who just got lost.

Looking down at her sleeping form, I watch her sleep. She looks so peaceful and content right now.

"Stop staring at me, you creeper," she huskily says, her voice laced with sleep.

"How did you know I was? Your eyes are closed."

"I could feel your gaze on me."

"Can you feel this too?" I ask, rolling to my side, I thrust my morning wood into her thigh but it backfires on me when with her eyes closed, she grips my cock in her hand

and begins to stroke. "Fuck me," I moan and she squeezes me tighter and tighter with each flick of her wrist. "Kitten, if you keep that up, I'm going to come and I would much rather do that inside of you."

"Mouth or pussy?" she taunts me.

"I don't care. I just need to be inside you...now."

Quicker than I've ever seen her move, she rolls on top of me and slides down my shaft, impaling herself. She purrs in that sexy way she does when she's aroused. "Fuck, hurry up, Kitten. I'm ready to burst."

She rocks her hips back and forth. With one hand, she tugs on her nipple, and with the other, she circles her clit before gently tugging on her piercing. When she does this, I feel her walls tighten around me. "Now," I grunt and together, the two of us tumble over the orgasmic cliff.

She opens her eyes and stares down at me, "Good morning, Agent Cox."

I fucking love hearing her call me that. Reaching up, I cup her boob and gently massage the plump mound. "Morning, Ms. Evans," I say, as I sit up and wrap my arms around her.

"Kitten, my name is Kitten to you."

"Duly noted." Leaning forward, I take her nipple into my mouth and suck. She moans and circles her hips, my dick coming back to life even though I just came moments ago. Letting the taut peak pop out of my mouth, I gaze into her vibrant blue eyes. "Should I fuck you again? Or feed you?"

"Fuck, then feed." Her breathing is heavy. Her hips rocking back and forth, her pace increasing the longer we stare at one another. Her movements are slow and sensual. Our gazes fused to one another as we both rock backward and forward.

"I need more," she pleads. Leaning forward, I take her nipple into my mouth and suck. Gently biting the tip before sucking again. "Yes," she mewls, as our movements increase.

She grips my cheeks and slams her lips to mine. Her tongue plunges into my mouth as she rides my cock. Sex just gets better and better with her. She bites my lip and it sets me off, out of nowhere, I erupt inside of her. We haven't once used a condom but I don't give a flying fuck. I'd happily have a million kids with Baylor Evans.

"Coooooorey," she roars as she, too, climaxes.

We stop moving and with my forehead against hers, we both get our breathing under control.

A knock on the bedroom door startles us, "Corey, I need to speak with you," Charli says.

"Give me a sec!" I shout back.

"Okay, meet me in the kitchen," she says, and then we hear her footsteps as she walks away.

Baylor and I stare at one another and for the first time in twelve hours, she looks frightened. "What's wrong, Kitten?"

"It's nothing," she denies, but I can tell from the look on her face, it's something.

"Don't deny it, missy, it's written all over your face. What's wrong?"

"Hearing Charli, it brought me back to reality. I'm in WitSec 'cause my crazy ex is trying to kill us. After this is over, who knows what will happen."

"What do you want to happen after all this is over?"

She stares blankly at me. Her mouth opens and closes a few times. "Don't answer me now. Think about what you want and when you know, let me know." I cup her cheek in my palm, she snuggles into it and stares at me. "But I will confirm, I want this. I want you. Any way you'll have me."

"Naked and on a beach?"

"Sure. After this, I'll take you to a tropical oasis and we can do exactly that."

"I'd like that." She climbs off me. "I'm going to take a shower. You go chat to Charli." She stands up and grabs her robe. Pulling it on, she looks at me over her shoulder. "And, Corey," I look up at her, "I want you any way you'll have me, too."

Before I can reply, she opens the door and steps into the bathroom across the hall.

Climbing out of bed, I re-dress and head to the kitchen to meet Charli and Dean. Dean looks pissed off. I wonder what's crawled up his ass but before I can say anything, he pushes his chair back, "I'm doing a perimeter check." He storms out of the kitchen, slamming the door behind him.

"Was it something I said?" I say to Charli, as I pour myself a coffee.

"Beats me. He needs to pull his head out of his ass and start pulling his weight."

"What do you mean? He's doing the perimeter checks, what more should he be doing?"

"Actually checking it for starters, I watched him last night from my room upstairs. He walked down the drive and that's all he did. He was on his phone, not doing his job. I called him out on it, and now he's got his panties in a twist."

"Is that normal for him?" I question, as I take a seat at the dining table across from her.

"Lately, yes. It's like his mind is elsewhere. Anyway, I wanted to discuss further what we talked about yesterday."

"What about it?"

"Are you okay with the changes made?"

"I'm fine with it and I think, Bay is too."

"Bay hey? What happened to Ms. Evans?"

"Ohh, piss off. You know perfectly well that our relationship has changed. It's…"

"Complicated?" she offers.

"Well, yes that, but I was more thinking along the lines of the start of something."

"No shit," she scoffs, "I never thought I'd see the day that Corey Cox finds 'the one' and focuses on something other than work." She air quotes 'the one' and I find myself grinning when I realize she might be right. From the moment I saw Baylor, I knew she was special. "It's nice to see you relaxing while us mere mortals are slaving away keeping you safe."

"Ohh piss off, Davis. This is just as much of a holiday for you as it is for me. It's not often you get stationed in the woods by a gorgeous lake like this. How did you pull that off?"

"I didn't. Dean did. He's the one who planned and signed off on the location and logistics. It was nice to see him step up for a change. Just wish he'd step up now that we're here."

"You need to chillax, Charli. Grab a book and sit out on the deck and enjoy the day."

"Where's Corey Cox and what have you done with him? The Corey I know is a workaholic, I fully expected you to demand a shift and to be involved in the day-to-day operations while being here."

I shrug at her. "What can I say, I'm a changed man."

"I think it has something to do with a certain blonde-haired, blue-eyed chick who is also living here." She pauses. "It's nice to see you smiling and relaxed for once."

"I smile," I retort.

She laughs at me. "Dude, before, you looked like Arnie in the Terminator movies when he'd smile or like you were constipated. Now, you actually smile, like a normal person."

"There's lots to smile about, now."

She shakes her head, "Whatever the reason, I'm happy. And I'm going to take your advice. I'm going to fill my coffee mug and go sit outside in the sun and read."

"Sounds like a plan."

Following her into the kitchen, I grab a mug and fill it up for Baylor. Charli heads outside. Grabbing the tub of taffy and her coffee, I head down to the hallway toward her room.

Stepping inside her room, my heart sinks when I see the window open and no sign of Baylor.

CHAPTER 31

Baylor

WITH A PEP IN MY STEP, I skip over to the bathroom. Pulling open the shower door, I reach into the cubicle and turn the faucets on, letting the water heat and steam up the room.

Looking at my reflection in the mirror, I smile. I look well fucked and rested, and it couldn't be more true. Last night was everything I dreamed it would be and more. Grabbing my toothbrush, I squeeze on some toothpaste and begin brushing. My mind drifts to last night and this morning, and my body comes alive at the memory.

Spitting out, I rinse my mouth and grab some mouthwash. Swishing it around, I climb into the shower where scalding water feels amazing on my body. I haven't had a workout like that in a very long time. Cox has some stamina, that's for sure.

Grabbing my bodywash, I lather up. Looking out, I see a silhouette through the frosted glass door. He doesn't realize I know he's here so I decide to play with him...and myself. I bend down, like they taught me at the pole dancing class I once took. My ass points in the air. When I straighten back up, I run my hands up my body. He will be able to see what I'm doing, and I hope it's turning him on as much as it's turning me on.

Turning to face him, I press myself against the frosted glass, squishing my breasts. The cool glass pebbles my nipples, and I gently tug and an illicit moan slips through my lips. Stepping back, I slide my hands down my body, flicking my clit ring and letting out another groan. I can't wait any longer, pushing on the door, I poke my head out and my eyes widen, "What the fuck?" I snarl, when I realize that I just did a sexy shower show for Dean.

"He said you were a kinky slut," he says, gripping his dick.

"Who did?"

"You know who." I stare at him blankly, I have no fucking clue who he's referring to but before I can question him further, he turns and leaves me staring at his retreating form. He quietly closes the door behind him. I stare at the wood for a few moments and shake my head in confusion.

Stepping under the spray, I rinse off and step out. Grabbing the fluffy purple towel, I dry off. Realizing I didn't bring any clothes in with me, I wrap the towel back around me, and step into my bedroom. I quickly pull on my jeans and a purple tank top. Sitting on the edge of the bed, I slip on my, you guessed it, purple Chucks.

After tying the laces, I fall back onto the mattress and sigh. Why was Dean in the bathroom just now? And who was he referring to? Surely Corey wouldn't have told him about last night, those two hate each other. And their hate is why I will be keeping this little peep show a secret. No good will come from Corey knowing what happened.

The room feels stuffy so I walk over to the window and open it. Looking out, I smile at the gorgeous sunny day before me. I'd love to go sit at the end of the jetty but Charli has forbidden that. Then I remember seeing a swing on the front porch. I grab my Kindle and climb out of the window. I don't want to run into Dean right now, I'm embarrassed at what he witnessed.

Taking a seat on the swing, I push off and relax back into the cushions. I'm up to the part in *Benched* where shits gonna hit the fan but before I get to the good part, I hear Corey screaming. He's yelling that I've been taken.

Standing up, I walk to the front door but it's locked. I can hear them inside so I walk around the side of the cabin and enter through the kitchen.

"He's taken her!" I hear Corey shout at Charli. "How the fuck did he find us here?"

Charli sees me and relaxes but Cox is still unaware I'm behind him and okay.

"Corey," Charli says, but he's in his own head mumbling to himself.

"She's a fighter. She's gonna be okay. We'll find her." He runs his hands through his hair. Even with his back to me, I can feel the concern radiating off him.

"Cox!" Charli shouts. She steps over to him, grips his chin, and turns his head toward me. His eyes land on mine and they instantly fill with relief.

"Kitten," he breathlessly says, as he stalks over to me, wrapping me tightly in his arms, and hugging to his chest. "Where were you? I was so scared." He pulls back and grips my cheeks but before I can answer him, he presses his lips to mine. He breaks the kiss and rests his forehead against mine.

"Calm your tits," I tell him, "I—"

"Do not tell me to calm my tits." He steps back from me and runs his fingers through his hair. I've noticed he does this when he's frustrated. "When I walked into your room and saw the window opened and you nowhere in sight, I panicked."

"Overreact much?"

"Not when there's a fucking psychopath on the loose trying to kill us both I'm not."

I can't help it and I roll my eyes. He shakes his head. "I knew you were trouble when you walked in, but you know what?"

"What?" I quietly whisper, unsure of what he's about to say.

"The first time I looked into your eyes, I knew underneath your bitchy, snarky exterior was a girl wanting to be loved and be accepted for who she is, warts and all." He pauses. "No one is perfect, Kitten. I know I'm certainly not, but it's how we act that decides if we are worthy and you, Baylor Evans, are worthy."

"You are so full of shit, Cox. You're perfect, me? Not so much."

He shakes his head. "If only you could see what I see."

"What do you see?"

Stepping over to me, he cups my cheek and whispers, "You."

That one word is laced with so much, no one has spoken to me like this before—ever. No one has said that about ME before. My eyes well with tears. This can't be my life. This doesn't happen to people like me. I feel like I'm in a movie, or a dream, right now because this clearly is not real. Never has anyone professed their like for me as Corey just did. Ave? Yes. Me? Nope, no way in hell.

A tear breaks free. He swipes it away with the pad of his thumb. "Why are you crying, Kitten?"

"I...I, no one has ever said that to me before. I've never, I..." I'm really confused right now, hence my gibberish. "Are you sure?"

"Sure about what?"

"That you like me? I think you have blood loss, or you hit your head while we were fucking last night and you have a brain injury."

He laughs and I find myself laughing with him. "You really are something, Baylor Evans, but I promise you, every word I just spoke is true."

"Really?"

"Really, really. Now come here and kiss me."

"You come here and kiss me," I tease back. Raising my eyebrows at him.

"With pleasure." He closes the distance between us, grips my cheeks, and presses his lips to mine.

A sniffle from behind us garners our attention. We pull apart and look over at Charli who's wiping at her eyes. "You all right, Davis?" Corey asks her.

"Yeah, got a bug in my eye. I'm going to get back to my book outside. Leave you two lovebirds alone." She walks past us, grinning. The door closes behind her and it's just Corey and me.

"Sooo," I offer. "What now?"

"Promise me you won't scare me again like that?"

"Promise. I didn't mean to scare you, Core." His smile widens suddenly. "Why are you grinning like the cat who caught the canary?"

"You called me Core."

"And?" I ask him, genuinely confused right now.

"I usually hate when people call me Core, but when you say it, I kinda like it."

"Look at us, evolving. I like it when you call me Kitten and you like me calling you Core. Kitten and Core, a match made in WitSec."

"Leave the WitSec part out and it's perfect."

"My life hasn't been perfect in a very long time."

"Well, Kitten, this is only just the beginning."

CHAPTER 32
Baylor

...five weeks later

TIME IS SOMEHOW FLYING by but at the same time, it's dragging on. Corey and my relationship is moving along in leaps and bounds. I've never been in a relationship like this before. He's so attentive but more than that, he can read me like a book. He knows when I'm down and he knows exactly how to turn my frown upside down.

"Morning, Kitten," he says, as he enters the kitchen. He's shirtless and sweat covers him. Even all sweaty and gross, he's the sexiest man I've ever laid eyes on.

"Morning, Core," I say, as I hand him a cool glass of water. Our fingers brush and like every time we touch, an electrical current flies through my body. "I don't know why I can't go for a run with you."

"You know why," he tells me, as he finishes his water. We have this argument each time he goes for a run.

"You're in just as much danger as I am."

"Don't argue with me, Kitten."

"But—"

"No buts, don't make me handcuff you, Kitten."

"Maybe I want to be handcuffed," she throws back at me.

"It can be arranged but unlike the spankings you so enjoy, you won't enjoy this."

"Wanna make a bet?" I sass, resting my hand on my hip and cocking it to the side. The material on my sundress pulls down, revealing the top of my breasts. His eyes drop to my chest and darken with lust. He lifts his heated gaze back to mine.

"Don't tempt me, Kitten."

I wink at him and sashay out of the room. Looking over my shoulder, I notice his eyes are on my ass, so I add an extra swing as I walk away. I step into the bathroom and from the other room, I hear Corey murmur, "Fuck me." I bet he's sitting there, running his hands over his face in frustration.

An idea forms in my head and with a grin on my face, I duck into my bedroom. With everything I need in hand, I head back out. He's still on the sofa and he's resting his elbows on his knees with his head down. He's so lost in thought he doesn't hear me return, which is perfect for what I have in mind.

Silently, I snap one side of the handcuffs around my wrist and then the other to his wrist. His gaze lifts to mine in shock. "Oops," I cheekily say, "did I do that?" That's when he notices I'm only wearing a sheer purple teddy. *Thank you Ave for including this in my care package.*

"What happened to your dress?"

"I took it off," I nonchalantly say, as I push him back onto the sofa and straddle his thighs. "Now, since we are cuffed, and alone, I think we should have some fun."

"I'm listening," he tells me, his gaze locked on mine.

"Well, since you are attached to me, literally and figuratively, I thought..." I stop talking and trail my fingertip over his chest, letting my fingers to the talking.

"You thought what?"

With my eyes on his, I keep moving my finger over his chest. Sliding lower and lower. Tracing my finger along the top of his cargos, I lean closer. My breasts pressing into his chest, I take his earlobe into my mouth and nibble. "I thought we could explore each other's bodies with our hands and tongue and teeth."

"I'm down with that but I have one amendment."

"I don't think you are in a position to bargain but I'm open to suggestions," I breathe heavily into his ear, garnering a groan from him.

"Do you trust me?" he pants.

Pulling back to stare at him, I reply honestly, "With my life."

"Good," he says and before I know it, he lifts me into his arms bridal style and walks us into the bedroom. He lays me down on the bed and cocoons me, pressing his lips to mine and kissing the life out of me. I'm so lost in the kiss I don't realize what he's doing. He laced our fingers together and unbeknownst to me, he slipped the cuff off his wrist and now I'm attached to the bed via the cuffs, with my arms stretched above me.

"What the?"

"You should know better than that, Kitten. I will always win." He stares down at me and my body heats just from his gaze. "Now, what shall I do with you?"

"I have a few ideas," I tell him.

"Uh uh, I'm in charge now."

He climbs off the bed and ever so slowly he removes his pants, followed by his boxer briefs. Once he's naked, he stands beside the bed and stares down at me, languidly stroking his cock.

"If you uncuff me, I can do that for you."

"You can also help me while cuffed, you have a perfectly good mouth."

"Well then, come here." I lick my lips and open wide, waiting for his cock.

"Ohh, Kitten," he says, resting a knee on the edge of the mattress. He continues to stroke his cock, while my clit pulsates with need.

"Shut the fuck up, Core, and shove your cock in my mouth."

"Yes, ma'am."

"Don't fucking call me ma'am."

"Watch your mouth, Kitten."

"Fill my mouth with your cock and you can watch it for me."

He straddles me and taps his cock against my chin, smearing precum on my skin. I'm about to protest again when he thrusts his hips forward and his cock passes between my lips. It hits the back of my throat causing me to gag a little. As he moves his hips back and forth, I pucker my cheeks and suck as best as I can. "Fuck, Kitten, your mouth feels like heaven."

When he stares down at me, I have never felt more wanted or desired in my life. His cock twitches and I know he's close to coming. Gently, I graze my teeth on his shaft. He hisses and then I feel the first hot spurt hit the back of my throat and I suck every last drop from him. He removes his cock from my mouth and leans forward and shoves his tongue into my mouth, kissing me deeply.

His hand slides down my side. My skin prickles at his light touch. Slipping his hand between my thighs, he cups me. "Kitten, you're soaked," he murmurs against my lips. "What should we do about that?"

"Fuck me," I tell him, my body is on the edge right now. He doesn't move, but I'm ready to combust. "Fu—" But I don't get to finish my curse because he thrusts two fingers inside me. My heads drops back and I give myself and my pleasure over to him. He kisses and nips down my neck toward my breasts. Massaging them, he continues to finger fuck me. My orgasm is just about there but as soon as I feel like I'm about to explode, the asshole stops moving his fingers.

"Corey," I beg when he starts to move them again. "I need to come."

"Not until I say so," he tells me.

He uses his knuckle and nudges my piercing with each outward stroke. My body is buzzing with the need to come. My walls clench around his fingers and just before I explode, he slides down my body and sucks my piercing into his mouth. That suction sets me off and I come harder than I ever have before. He continues to shove his fingers in and out and suck on my clit as I come and come and come. Finally, my body relaxes and I recline into the mattress.

"Holy shit," I pant.

Corey lifts his head from between my thighs, his chin glistening with my arousal. Beckoning himself forward, he crawls up my body and hovers over me. "Kiss me," I demand.

"Yes, ma'am." And before I can protest at him calling me ma'am, he presses his lips to mine and slides his tongue into my mouth. We kiss like teenagers at the drive-in on a Saturday night, but unlike teenagers, we make it through all the bases and he hits a home run. Corey slides into me and fucks me slowly. His cock moving in sync with his tongue in my mouth.

Corey and I languidly make love to one another. This is definitely making love because it's slow and sensual. It's perfect in every way possible. Together we come, moaning into each other's mouths. We continue to kiss and eventually, we fall asleep. Corey on my chest and me still cuffed to the bed.

Startling awake after a nightmare, I realize I'm alone. Corey must have uncuffed me while I was sleeping. Looking at the clock on the side table, I realize it's late afternoon. Slipping my dress and underwear back on, I cross the hall to the bathroom and freshen up.

Looking at my reflection in the mirror, I don't recognize the woman staring back at me. There's life in my eyes and for the first time in a long time, I realize I'm happy and I'm falling in love. Splashing water on my face, I wipe it dry and head into the kitchen for a drink.

With my drink in hand, I head out the front door and sit on the porch swing. Tucking my legs underneath me, I rub at my wrist. It's a little chaffed from our sexcapades earlier. I think if, no, when, we do that again, we'll need to get a fuzzy pair of cuffs to prevent chaffing.

"What's got you grinning?" Charli asks me as she walks up the front stairs.

"Nothing," I say.

She sits down and turns to face me. "I call bullshit and from the red marks and moaning I heard earlier, I'd say you're on a sex high."

"Maybe," I nonchalantly shrug at her. She eyes me. "Okay, yes, I'm on a sex high."

"Again," she teases. "I'm so happy and not jealous at all."

"I'm sorry."

"No, you're not."

"Yeah, you're right, I'm not really that sorry. You could always hook up with Dean."

She scrunches her face and shakes her head, "Hard pass there. He's my partner in a work sense and that's all it will ever be. Plus, he's not really my type."

"What IS you type?" I ask her.

"Not him," she laughs. "I don't know. I've been married to my job for so long now, I haven't really had time for a relationship or love."

"I get that but you really need to look out for yourself, too. You're a hot chick; don't you want that giddy feeling when they're near? Or the happiness that comes from being with someone?"

"Can't say I've ever had that. Not sure I'm cut out for love."

"I bet you will meet someone one of these days and when you do, it will be love at first sight and you will fall hard and fast."

"Yeah, I wouldn't bet on that."

"Never say never," I tell her.

We both fall silent and I can see our chat racing through her mind. Standing, I look down at her. "It's Tuesday, you know what that means?"

Together we singsong, "It's Taco Tuesday."

Linking arms, we head inside and begin prepping dinner.

After a delicious taco dinner, sans margaritas—damn WitSec and no alcohol—Corey and I spend the rest of the evening in my room, devouring each other's bodies like we do most nights and I fall asleep in his arms, blissfully happy.

Waking the next morning, I stretch out my muscles from head to toe. My body aches in the most delicious way. A noise startles me and I quickly sit up. My Spidey senses are on high alert. "Corey?" I yell but I'm met with silence. That feeling of unease increases.

Staring up, I pull on my robe when the door to my room swings open. My heart stops beating when I see who's standing there; they were the last people I expected to see.

CHAPTER 33

Kye

SOON EVERYTHING I've worked so hard for will be in place. Sure, my base of operations has been taken to another country but I'm Kye fucking Vlahos, no one can bring me down. *She* and the feds tried, but I'm like a cat with nine lives.

The door opens and Monica slides into the seat next to me. Just as the door closes, my driver pulls away from the curb. She turns her head and stares at me. "It's all arranged."

"Excellent," I tell her.

There's hunger in her eyes and I know she'll do anything I ask of her. Right now, I need her more than she needs me, but she's so clueless she doesn't realize I'm using her to get what I want, Baylor Evans. She is my one true queen and even though she betrayed me, she will rule by my side. I will make sure of it...and I know exactly how to make her comply.

Grabbing my phone, I scroll through my contacts list and when I get to the one I'm after, I click their name. "What?" he growls on the second ring.

"It's time."

"I told you, I don't have it yet."

"I have a new repayment in mind. Give me what I need now and we'll call it even."

"I'm listening," he tells me. I can hear the desperation in his voice but when you have nothing to live for, you look after number one. Consequences be damned.

"I need an address."

"An address?" he repeats with confusion and as soon as the penny drops, he mumbles, "Ohh."

"Ohh, indeed."

"I'll tell you what you need but you need to promise me something."

"You aren't really in a position to be bargaining with me."

"If you want that address you need to guarantee me that she won't be harmed."

"Which 'she' are we referring to?"

"You know who I'm referring to. Guarantee me her safety and not only will I get you an address, but I'll help you secure the package."

This is a change of events I didn't see coming and it can work to my advantage if I let him think he's in control. "You have a deal. Two days and it's all going down."

"Why wait?"

His eagerness to get this over with shows his desperation. Looking to Monica, she nods her head that she can move up her timeframe. "Tomorrow, lunchtime," I confirm and then I hang up. "You sure you can get it done sooner?"

"Do you not trust me?"

"No, I don't. I don't trust anyone, Monica. And I especially don't trust anyone without a penis between their thighs."

"Sexist much?" she scoffs, crossing her arms and pushing her tits up. She's not wearing a bra under her dress; she's such a fucking slut.

Leaning over, I trace my fingertip across the hem of her dress, sliding my hand under the material and cupping her tit. Squeezing her nipple painfully between my thumb and forefinger, I pull the flimsy material down and suck the tip into my mouth. She reaches across, grabs my cock, and begins to stroke. Gripping the back of her neck, I throw her to the floor and like the good little slut she is, she pulls out my cock and begins to suck. This woman sucks like a Hoover and before long, I'm coming down her throat. Like always, I imagine it's Baylor sucking me off and her name passes through my lips as I empty my load down Monica's throat.

"Did you just moan that bitch's name while you came?" she asks, wiping at her lips.

"Yep," I honestly tell her. "Just like I imagine it's her every time."

"You're a fucking asshole. That whore betrayed you and you still want her. What makes her so special?"

"She isn't you and the fact you can't see it says it all." I tell her, "Now, I suggest you pull your panties out of your cunt and concentrate on the plan." I stare intently down at her. "Don't fuck this up for me, otherwise you will meet a nasty demise. Am I clear?"

"Crystal," she huffs, sliding back into the seat next to me. I think about what she said, she's right, Baylor did betray me and that betrayal is why I want her by my side. She will be miserable for the rest of her days and that's the best form of punishment.

"Good," I tell her, looking out of the window, I watch the city fly by. Tomorrow everything will change. My queen will be back by my side and the future will be mine, but first, I need to tidy up a few loose ends.

Dropping Monica off at her practice, I head to the ware-house and swap cars. I sit in my car and watch. I've been following her, biding my time and finally, that time is here. I didn't get to where I am from making rash decisions. No, I got here because I'm meticulous and plan everything methodically. Sure, I didn't plan on *her* betraying me, that blindsided me, but I will not let that happen again.

Like clockwork, they step onto the street. She kisses him goodbye and walks down the street. He heads back inside and in three minutes, he will pull out of the underground parking lot. Like clockwork, his car pulls onto the street and he drives off, leaving me acess to his most prized possession.

Driving down the street, I pull into the side alley. Climbing out of my car, I wait. I hear her steps getting closer. Stepping onto the sidewalk, I stop in front of her. She stops and looks up at me. She stares at me and the moment it clicks as to who I am, she scoffs and turns to run, but I was waiting for that.

Grabbing her, I pull her into me and start walking toward my car. "Hello, Avery," I whisper into her ear. Opening the back door, I grab the syringe filled with Propofol, and inject it into her neck.

Shoving her inside, I look down at her. Her eyes are getting heavy and before she passes out, I tell her, "Let's go see your bitch of a sister."

CHAPTER 34

Corey

WAKING up next to Baylor is fast becoming a habit and the best way to wake up. I can count on one hand the number of times in the last five weeks I've slept in my room. Quietly climbing out of bed, I pull on my sweats and shirt and head into the kitchen.

Looking up, I'm surprised when I see Dean standing at the back door, looking out into the yard. He hasn't heard me enter the kitchen, some WitSec agent he is. "Morning," I say, startling him, the reaction is odd but then again, it's Dean. He is odd.

"Hey," he says, and then turns his attention back outside. "Doing my morning check, back soon." He opens to door and heads outside, leaving me alone.

The smell of coffee hits my nose and I smile. *At least the asshole made coffee*, I think to myself as I grab a mug and pour a cup. Taking a sip, I moan as the caffeine hits my bloodstream. With my mug in hand, I step out the kitchen door and walk toward the stairs down to the backyard when out of my peripheral vision, I see two men near the tree line. Turning my head, my eyes widen when I see it's Kye Vlahos and Dean. The two of them are standing there having a conversation like two old chums catching up.

A creak on the decking boards turns my attention away from them. Turning around, I see a woman standing there. When she sees me, she lunges at me and injects something into my neck. Dropping my mug, I take a few steps backward and begin to tumble down the stairs. Landing on my back with a thud, a shadow appears above me but the drug injected combined with my fall blurs my vision. Darkness engulfs me and I pass out.

When I come too, I realize my hands are tied behind my back. Next to me, someone sniffles. Turning my head, I'm relieved to see Baylor. "Kitten," I say, my voice croaky. "Are you okay?"

"I'm Ave," she says and my heart drops. "I'm okay, but where is she? Where's Bay?"

"You'll see her soon enough…" Kye says, and then adds, "maybe."

"Let Avery go. She has nothing to do with this."

"No, she doesn't, but it's so much fun messing with people. That bitch fucked with me so I'm going to fuck with her, but mark my words, Agent Cox, after today, Baylor will be mine and not yours."

"Over my dead fucking body," I snarl, trying to break free from the ropes currently binding my wrists behind my back.

"That's the plan," he growls. Raising his fist, he punches me in the face. My head snaps back, colliding with the railing.

From beside me, Avery begins to sob. "Shhhh, it's okay, Avery."

"How? And where's Bay?"

"My queen is still sleeping," Kye tells us, "She'll need her sleep for what I have planned for her."

"What are you going to do to her? To us?" Avery asks him.

"I can't tell you everything. There needs to be some mystery in this. We just need to find Agent Davis and then the games can begin."

Shit, Charli. She hadn't even entered my mind. Late last night she was summoned to the city so she left after dinner. When she gets back here, she'll be walking into an ambush. I need to get loose and get Avery and Baylor out of here. Their safety is my one and only priority.

"Don't even think about it, Cox. You are at my mercy. Don't try and play hero, otherwise you'll end up dead sooner. Actually, go for it. I can't wait to end you."

Dean jumps up from his spot near the stairs, knocking over the trash can. In the quiet of the morning, it echoes loudly. Piercing the serenity.

"You all right there, heffalump?"

"There was a bug," he whines like the little bitch he is and I can't help but laugh. This pisses him off. He storms over to me and in quick succession punches me in the face. "You're a fucking dead man," he snarls.

"Enough!" Kye bellows, when from inside we hear Baylor yell my name. A sinister smile appears on his face, "It's showtime."

He roughly grabs Avery and drags her inside. Tears are pouring down her face, and she keeps tripping over her feet as the fear in her increases. I'm helpless to do anything. The kitchen door closes behind them and I'm left with a psychotic Dean and the woman who injected me earlier.

From the corner of my eye, I see Charli through the veranda railing. She stares at me and the scene before her. She mouths something to me but I miss what she says because the kitchen door swings open. She ducks down out of sight. Kye steps onto the deck, pushing Avery and Baylor in front of him. He's using them as a shield in case he's been caught.

A laugh escapes me. "What the fuck are you laughing at, asshole?" Dean growls.

"Big bad Kye Vlahos is using two women as a shield. He's a fucking pansy."

He shoves Baylor and Avery to the side and storms over to me and pulls out a pistol, pressing it to my temple. A feminine scream pierces the quiet of the morning. We all look over to Baylor who is currently walking toward him. "If you love me at all, Kye, you will not pull that trigger."

"What makes you think I still love you?"

She stops in front of him and cups his cheek; that contact makes my blood boil. She stares at him, just like she did the day of the takedown all those months ago, and I suddenly feel like she's been playing me this whole time. That she was just biding her time for *him* to come and rescue her.

She looks to me and smirks. "I'm Baylor fucking Evans, everyone fucking loves me."

Eight words is all it takes for my world to coming crashing down around me and confirm my fear. She used me.

CHAPTER 35

Baylor

WHEN I SAY THOSE WORDS, my world around me comes crashing down. Corey actually believes I've turned and that hurts me to my core. Before I can try and clue him in that it's all a ruse, Kye slides his arm around my waist and slams his lips to mine. I'm shocked and when my mouth opens, he shoves his tongue inside. My eyes close and a tear falls free.

"Fuck, I've missed those lips," Kye tells me.

I smile at him; it's all I can manage right now. From next to me, Ave cries and that sound snaps me back to the present. Looking around, I need to figure a way out, and I'm positive the only way to do so is to continue this charade with Kye.

Lacing my fingers with his, I squeeze his hand. "Let's get out of here," I tell him and I try to drag him away.

"Bay, what are you doing?" Ave pleads.

Looking to her, I see it in her eyes, disappointment. I wish I could tell her I love her. That I'm doing this to save them but I can't right now. As much as it pains me, I need them to think I've turned. Their safety hinges on this.

"Not so fast. Before we go, you have a choice to make."

"And what choice might that be?"

"Her or him?"

"Excuse me?" I question him, but I think I already know.

"In order for us to leave, someone needs to die. You, as my queen get to choose."

Dean grabs Ave and marches her over to Corey. He pushes her to her knees and roughly squeezes her shoulder. My eyes well with tears as my gaze flicks between the two most important people in my life. No matter what I do right now, someone I love will die.

From behind me, a woman laughs. Looking over my shoulder, I see Monica fucking Quinn. I'm not surprised at all that she's here, helping him. She's a fucking scum, I was no better before I started all this but now, I've changed. I'm not the selfish bitch I used to be and that's why this choice is impossible.

"She can't choose, Kye, because she loves him. It's written all over her face." Monica sneers, "She never loved you, not like I do. I'm your true queen, Kye. Give me that gun and I'll prove how much I'm yours. I'll kill—"

A gunshot rings out and I look over to see Monica collapse to the deck. Looking back at Kye in shock, I'm sick to my stomach when I see the sinister look on his face.

"No one threatens my queen or tells me what to do." He looks to me and cups my cheek. "Now, who do you choose?"

"I…I…" I can't answer him. I don't want either of them to die. I can't live without either one of them. I just can't.

"Time's up, bitch," he snarls at me. "Time to choose who lives…and who dies."

Looking back to Kye, I stare into his evil eyes and that's when my decision hits me. "Me," I whisper.

"Sorry, I didn't hear that."

Taking a step closer to him, I stare at him. "I. Choose. Me," I confidently say, enunciating each word to prove my point. My voice is strong and confident; the complete opposite of how I really feel, but it's the only way to protect them both. It's a sacrifice I'm willing to make because I realize in this moment; I love him. This will be my ultimate act of love.

"I love you," I murmur. Turning my head, I stare at Corey and smile. "I love you." Turning my gaze to Ave, I swallow back a sob. "I love you too, Ave."

"You love him?" Kye snarls, grabbing my shoulder roughly, spinning me to face him.

"Yes!" I shout at him. "I love him with every fiber of my being, therefore to save them, I chose me. I'd rather be dead than spend a day breathing at your side without one of them here. Kye, you don't get to dictate my life anymore. I make my own decisions and I choose me!" I shout, "You were the worst decision I've ever made. I give my life for theirs, it's the ultimate sacrifice I can make."

"And it's one more shitty decision you've made, Baylor." He raises his pistol and points it directly at me. My heart is racing but as I stare down the barrel of the gun in Kye's hand, I know I'm doing the right thing. The click of the safety causes me to jump. Taking a deep breath, I close my eyes. I'm ready for death but as with everything in my life, it doesn't go according to plan.

Kye sneers and it hits me, he's not going to just kill me; he's going to kill them too. I've just fucked this up for everyone, but before I can come up with a plan, gunshots pierce through the silence. The sound of the gunfire is deafening. My ears are ringing; everything is muffled. Everything happens in slow motion.

I'm frozen on the spot, staring into the distance when it comes roaring back to life. People are yelling. Feet are pounding on the deck. Someone is crying nearby and as I stand here, it suddenly hits me. I'm still alive.

Shaking my head, I look around at the chaos before me. I look down and my eyes widen. I gasp and cover my mouth. My eyes well with tears and everything, once again, becomes blurry.

The first tear drops and it causes an avalanche to flow behind them. I fall to my knees and stare into lifeless eyes.

Kye is dead.

Looking next to him, my heart stops when I see it's Corey lying next to him. His eyes are closed and there's a growing red spot on his chest. Vaguely, I hear Ave yelling my name, but I continue to stare at Corey. He's not moving. He's not breathing. There's so much blood and it continues to seep out of his chest.

Black spots hinder my vision.

Blinking becomes difficult.

Breathing hurts.

Everything becomes muffled.

My last thought before I drift into the dark abyss is that he's dead and I'm not, how will I live with that?

CHAPTER 36

Corey

OPENING MY EYES, I blink a few times. My shoulder is throbbing, my head is fuzzy, and there's an incessant beeping coming from the machine next to me. Looking to the side, I see someone in the chair by the window. My vision is quite blurry so I can't make them out clearly, but I can tell it's a woman.

Clearing my throat, I garner their attention. They sit up immediately and when they see me, they stand and walk over. I watch her as she walks over to me. My vision is still shit and I can't see her properly, but her eyes are a vivid blue. Her lips are moving but I can't hear what she's saying, it's muffled. Her form becomes blurrier. My eyelids become heavy. Blinking is difficult. I close my eyes and drift off into darkness again.

The next time I wake, my shoulder still hurts, my head is less heavy, the beeping is still loud, but this time my eyes stay open. The room comes into focus and I look to the chair but this time, there's a brunette sitting there. When she notices me staring at her, she stands. "About time you woke up, Sleeping Beauty."

"Very funny, Davis. What happened?"

"What do you remember?" she throws back at me.

"It's all hazy right now." I swallow but my mouth is drier than the Sahara desert right now. "Water," I croak out.

She grabs the pitcher from the rolling table and fills it up. She brings it to my lips and I drink. I gulp down the whole cup in a few seconds. "More."

She shakes her head, "Not too much, otherwise you'll be sick. You've been out for forty-eight hours now. Surgery went well."

"Surgery?" I question, but then I remember my shoulder, lifting my right hand I rub over it and missing pieces come back to me. A cabin by a lake. A man with a gun. Two women who look the same. Gunfire. Then nothing. "What happened?" I ask again.

"You were shot—"

"No shit," I fire back at her. "Who shot me?"

"Kye Vlahos," she says and then stares at me, not elaborating further.

That name is familiar but I can't quite place it. "Why do I know that name?"

"Because..." Again she doesn't say anything.

My mind is all jumbled right now. Closing my eyes, I lie back, and like a strike of lightning, I remember facing off with Kye. We were in a banquet room, but it was him who was shot in the shoulder. The woman from earlier was with him and that confuses me even more.

My head begins to throb, blood whooshing in my ears. The machine I'm attached to begins to erratically beep, much like the thudding of my heart right now.

The door to my room swings open and it's pandemonium. My body feels heavy and the darkness once again envelops me and I drift off.

This time, I dream of the blue-eyed woman. We are standing on the end of a jetty, a cabin behind us. I'm in black board shorts and she's wearing a purple string bikini and she looks fucking amazing. Taking her hand in mine, I pull her and we jump into the water. She wriggles free from me and swims away. She turns around and we stare intently at one another when a gunshot rings through the silence.

Turning my head, standing on the end of the dock, I see Kye Vlahos. His arm is outstretched and in his hand is a smoking gun. He's grinning and moves his gaze from mine and then he lets out a sinister laugh. Looking over, I see the woman floating in a pool of red bloody water. Another gunshot rings out but I wake with a start.

My heart is racing as I inhale deeply. "Fuck me," I moan, as the wound in my shoulder pulls from the deep breath I just took.

Lifting my right hand, I rub my fingers over my forehead. That dream felt so real but what I want to know is, why am I dreaming of this blue-eyed woman? And why was she here earlier? Maybe I dreamt that too.

The door to my room opens and in walks, Charli. She smiles when she sees me awake and walks over to take a seat next to my bed.

"Don't you ever do that again!"

"Do what?" I ask, genuinely confused. I'm in a hospital bed, what could I possibly have done?

"Flatline like you did. You scared the absolute shit out of me, Cox."

"My apologies. I'm sorry I got shot and my body decided to do whatever the hell it just did."

"Apology accepted. Now, how do you feel?"

"Like I got shot."

"Hardy fucking har."

"Watch your mouth, Davis." As soon as I say this, a warm and fuzzy feeling envelops me. I'm so confused right now. Nothing is making sense. "Can you fill me in, please?"

She takes a deep breath. "It seems that Dean was working with Vlahos and gave up our location, hence how he found us."

"I never trusted that fucker," I snarl.

"I did and it pisses me the fuck off that I didn't realize he'd turned. I knew something was up with him but I never thought he'd do this."

"Don't beat yourself up. I didn't even click, I just presumed he was being a dick 'cause he is one."

"Well, I'm the bigger dick because I didn't realize my partner was dirty. That was actually why I was called away that night."

"Thank fuck you were called away because had you not, the outcome would have been very different."

"The outcome was still shit. You got shot. Vlahos died. Dean got away. At least Baylor and Avery are now safe."

"Who're they?" I ask her, I don't know anyone by those names.

She looks at me, concern on her face. "You're messing with me, right? You know who they are."

I shake my head. "I have no clue who you're talking about."

We both fall silent and then the door to my room opens and in walks the blue-eyed woman from my dream. When she sees me awake, her face breaks out in the most beautiful smile. She races over to me and hugs me. "Core, I'm so glad you're awake. I was so worried." She pulls back and cups my cheek and stares at me.

"Who are you?" I ask and my question removes the smile from her face.

"Hardy har, Mr. Comedian," she says, reaching up to cup my cheek.

Shaking my head, I push her hand away and look to Charli. "Charli, who is she?"

"Core, it's me. Baylor. Your Kitten."

"I don't know you. I don't have a kitten. I hate cats." I stare at her, trying to remember her, but the first memory I have of her is when I woke earlier and then again when she appeared in my dream.

Quietly, I whisper, "I don't know you."

CHAPTER 37

Baylor

"I DON'T KNOW YOU. I don't have a kitten." Those words play on repeat as I turn away from him and exit his room. The tears fall as I walk down the corridor. Exiting the hospital, I lean against the building and slide down. The brick wall scratches and digs into my back as I fall to the ground and cry.

Resting my head on my knees, I sob my broken heart out.

He doesn't remember me.

I don't know how long I sit out here but when I have no more tears to cry, I stand up and decide to go home. I've taken two steps when the hairs on my neck prickle. Looking up, I see Corey and Charli standing in the doorway of the hospital. My first thought is why is he out of bed? He only woke up a few minutes ago but when I look around, I realize it's dark. Clearly I've been sitting here crying for much longer than I thought.

Our gaze connects and we silently stare at one another. I plead internally for him to recognize me, but he continues to stare through me. My heart breaks all over again at his blank stare. My chest tightens and I realize I've been holding my breath. I try to breathe but I can't. I'm literally breathless right now. The more I try to inhale, the more it hurts. The panic building within me increases which halts my breathing further. My vision begins to dot; I stumble and fall. My head connects with the cement and then nothing. I let the darkness engulf me because I have nothing to live for anymore. Without him, I am nothing.

When I stir, I realize I'm in a hospital bed. Even though I'm awake, I keep my eyes closed because when I open them, it will all be real. Corey won't remember me and I'll be all alone. At least if I stay asleep, I can pretend he didn't just destroy my heart and soul.

Two people are talking; it's Ave and Flynn. I can hear from the pain in her voice that she's worried about me. I don't want her to worry but I also don't want to wake up and not have him in my life anymore.

"Why did this happen?" Ave cries.

"It seems the shock from the last week became too much and it caused her to lose consciousness. Her vitals are good, Ave. Now we just wait for her body to reset and then she'll wake up."

"She's been out for twelve hours now. Why won't she wake up, Flynn?"

"She's been through a lot, babe, and with the Corey thing, it's all caught up with her, but her body is doing what it should. Trust me, I know what she needs right now."

"Well, I need her to wake up," she snaps at him. "Flynn, I can't lose her." Ave murmurs, "I can't lose my BayBay."

"You won't," I croak out. Hearing the sadness in her voice hurts too much, I can't pretend to still be asleep anymore. "I'm sorry," I tell her, as she sits on my bed and takes my hand in hers.

"Why are you apologizing?" Ave asks me, as she brushes my hair off my forehead.

"'Cause I made you worry, again," I quietly tell her.

"Bay, I will always worry," she confirms to me, and I can tell by the tone of her voice she means it.

Lifting my gaze to hers, my eyes well with tears. "He doesn't remember me," I tell her. A tear breaks free and then an avalanche follows behind. Ave pulls me into her embrace and I cry into her shoulder. The clicking of my door causes me to lift my head and I see that Ave and I are alone. "Ave, why doesn't he remember me?"

"Flynn said it's some sort of short-term memory amnesia, he remembers stuff from years ago but not recently." I sadly nod as I listen but all I hear is, he doesn't remember me. "But if it makes you feel better, while you were out, he came to visit."

"Not really but it's something. I guess."

"He seems upset, Bay. He was asking about your relationship, but Flynn said to not say too much otherwise it will confuse his mind and may block it permanently."

"I should have known that something like this would happen. I'm not destined for a happily ever after."

"Yes, you are," she says, squeezing my hand. "The past is in the past. You need to look to the future. Your future with Corey." She pauses and then adds, "And as a kick-ass aunty."

My mouth drops open and my eyes widen. "I'm going to be an aunty?"

She nods. "Yes, we found out yesterday. I have my first scan in a few weeks."

"Ohh, Ave," I cry, "I'm so happy for you." Pulling back, I look down at her belly, which looks a little pudgy up close. "Twins?"

She shrugs. "I don't know."

"I'm betting it's twin boys," I tell her as I lie back in my bed, smiling for the first time today. "You think you can grab me some—"

"Taffy and a coffee?"

"You know me so well."

"I sure do." She stands up and walks to the door, before she opens it, she looks over her shoulder, "It will all work out, Bay, I promise."

She exits my room and I stare at the closed door. I hope she's right because I really do love him. I hope I get my chance at happiness but as with everything in my life, the door to my room opens and once again, shit hits the fan.

CHAPTER 38

Corey

WHEN I SAW that Baylor woman collapse, my heart hurt for her. I don't remember her but it seems we know each other. No one is telling me shit and it's pissing me off. There's a knock on my door and it opens, that woman's twin, Avery, pops her head in. They are very similar but I can tell she's not her. She smiles that sad 'I'm sorry' smile. "Can I come in?" Nodding my head, she steps inside but stays by the door. "Just letting you know Bay is awake and everything is okay."

Relief at hearing she's okay floods my body. "That's great," I pause, "how…how is she?"

She steps farther into my room. "Confused. Sad. Upset. Feels she deserves this."

"Why would she deserve me not remembering her?"

She bites her bottom lip and an image of Baylor doing that flashes in my mind and I smile. "What did you just remember?" Avery asks me.

"Does she do that?" I question.

"Do what?"

"Bite her lip like that. It sparked a memory of her sitting on a kitchen counter doing that."

She smiles at me. "Yeah, she does. Would you like to see her again?"

"Yes. No. I don't know," I tell her, as I rub the back of my neck in frustration. "I don't want to upset her again. She ended up in here because of me."

"No." She shakes her head. "She ended up in here because she's been through hell."

"Because of me."

"No!" she shouts. "Because of Kye and Dean. It's not your fault, Corey. Please for me. For Bay, go and see her. If me biting my lip sparked something, maybe spending some time with her will spark more memories." She bites her lip again and a vision of Baylor with a lake behind her flashes before my eyes. "Look, I don't know you very well, but I know you are good for her and I know that deep down, you feel something for her. Please don't give up on her."

Before I can reply, she exits my room. Leaving me alone with my thoughts and visions of Baylor biting her lip. As I keep thinking about that, my heart beats faster. It's as if it knows who she is. "Fuck it," I mumble to the room.

Hopping out of bed, I slip my feet into my slippers and I go to see her, hoping Avery is right and something she says or does will reboot my memory.

Stopping outside her door, I take a deep breath but I hear a commotion on the other side. Stepping into the room, Dean is standing beside her bed. He has his back to me and hasn't noticed me yet. He's focused on Baylor, her eyes are locked to his and that's when I notice he has a knife in his hand.

I can't see his face but his shoulders are hunched tightly and his breathing is deep and erratic. He's on edge and completely unhinged, Baylor is in trouble.

"Get the fuck away from me, asshole," Baylor growls at him, and those seven words cause everything to come crashing back to me. I remember.

Watching her in the interrogation room.

Her sassy tongue the first time we spoke.

Kissing her in her kitchen.

Arresting her the day we took down Kye.

Seeing her for the first time in the lobby after her release.

Waking up next to her at the cabin.

Handcuffing her to the bed.

Sliding my cock into her.

Her lips around my cock.

The look on her face when she pops a piece of taffy into her mouth.

Her smile.

Her laugh.

I remember…everything.

"Watch your mouth, Kitten," I say, causing both of them to turn their heads toward me. They both have shocked looks on their faces. His filled with malice at my arrival, and hers in shock that I'm here and I called her Kitten.

"You remember?" she whispers.

Nodding my head, I smile. "Everything. I remember everything, Kitten."

Tears well in her eyes, I want nothing more than to take her into my arms and kiss those sassy pouty lips, but Dean turns to face me.

"Well, isn't this nice?" he sneers. "The happy lovebirds are reunited just before they die." He looks back to Baylor. "Kye was right, you are a fucking cunt." He turns his attention to me. "And you, Corey-fucking-Cox, are nothing but a waste of space." He steps toward me and I realize, I have no weapon and I'm recovering from being shot.

He takes another step closer; I back up and hit the wall. I'm trapped and have nowhere else to go. *This is not good*, I think to myself but at least he's focused on me and not my kitten.

His eyes widen and then he falls to the ground. Behind him, Baylor stands there with her dinner tray in her hands. "Take that, you stupid fucker," she says to his crumpled body.

Normally I'd want to scold her for swearing but she's right, the fucker deserved that and more. We stare at one another. She smiles at me and bites her bottom lip. A smile appears on my face at seeing that because I remember everything about the woman before me. All the feelings I have for her bubble to the surface and I need her in my arms.

At the same time, we lunge for one another. She jumps over his body and I step forward. She wraps her arms around my waist and I throw my good arm around her shoulders, pulling her into me. I breathe her in. "I remember," I whisper into her hair. "I remember everything."

"I thought I'd lost you," she blubbers into my chest.

"I will always find you, Kitten."

She lifts her gaze to mine, and I cup her cheek and bend down to kiss her. As soon as our lips touch, everything is right in the world once again. A groan from Dean pulls us apart, just as the door opens and Ave walks in. Her eyes widen when she sees Baylor in my arms and then she smiles. Her gaze drops and her eyes widen farther when she sees Dean on the ground. Without saying a word, she turns back around and exits the room, leaving Bay and me alone, with a moaning Dean.

A few moments later, the door opens again and Charli is there with a uniformed officer.

She looks to Dean, "Dean Chikatilo," she says, her voice wavering, "you are under arrest for the attempted murder o…" She reads him his rights, but all my attention is on the blue-eyed woman in my arms.

"Kitten, I'm so sorry I didn't remember you," I honestly tell her, cupping her cheek in my palm. She leans into it and rubs her cheek on my hand.

"You have nothing to be sorry for."

"Yes, I do. You're the best thing to have come into my life. There's no way in hell I could forget someone like you. I also need to apologize for not saying it sooner."

"Saying what?" she asks, her face scrunched in confusion.

"I love you, Baylor Evans."

Her mouth drops open in shock and then she smiles. I've never seen anything more stunning in my life.

"I love you too, Corey Cox."

She reaches up, grips my cheeks, and presses her lips to mine. Everything around me fades away. It's just my Kitten and me. We may have hated each other when we first met, but there's a fine line between love and hate, and a love fueled from hate like ours is the strongest of them all. And my kitten is the strongest person I know.

CHAPTER 39

Baylor

...three months later

COREY WENT BACK to work this week after being shot, his surgery, and rehabilitation. He's a shitty patient but after purchasing a pair of fuzzy handcuffs and a slutty nurse's outfit, he became a pliant and willing patient. I'm sure the sexy outfit and a prescription of BJ's, spankings, and handcuffing had something to do with it.

And me? Well, yesterday I enrolled in community college to do a degree in mixology. I start next semester and I'm excited for the adventure ahead. In the meantime, I will keep trying to pull Charli out of her funk. She and I are meeting up for drinks tomorrow night. She's devastated that her partner betrayed her, but what upsets her the most is that she didn't see it coming. She knew Dean was acting strange but she put it down to his hate for Corey. Never in her wildest dreams did she think he was working for Kye. We still don't know why he was helping him; the asshole is refusing to give anything away.

We spent the evening at Avery and Flynn's. Today they had another scan and as I guessed when she first told me, she's pregnant with twin boys. The four of us had a lovely dinner, we've decided to try and do this weekly, but sometimes Flynn will be absent due to his shifts. I'm so glad Avie and I are back to being twinsies and that Flynn and Corey get along so well.

Ave and I join the boys at the door. "Yeah, my Kitten got me good!" Corey says to Flynn with a smile on his face. Stepping beside him, he pulls me into his side and kisses my temple. "She's a wild one, but she's my wild one," Corey says to Flynn and Avery. His words make me smile but it's true, he got me good and I wouldn't have it any other way.

Corey and I are walking down the street toward his car after saying our goodbyes. Our fingers are laced and I've never been happier. Looking over to him, I grin.

"What?" he asks.

"I love you," I honestly tell him and it hits me, I want to be with him forever. Pulling on his hand, I stop us. "Core, marry me?"

"Come again?"

"Marry me? I love you. You love me. I want to be with you forever. Life is too short but I know without a doubt, I want to grow old and gray with you."

"Isn't the guy supposed to ask the girl?"

"Probably, but I don't give a flying fuck, and before you tell me to watch my mouth, I know, language. So what do you say, Agent Cox, will you marry me?"

He stares at me. He's silent and I begin to wonder if he doesn't want what I want when he finally breaks the silence. "Fuck yes, I'll marry you."

I can't resist. "Watch your mouth, Core."

"Great, it's started already. You bossing me around."

"Get fucked, fiancé," I sass at him, "Now take me home and ravage me. We have some celebrating to do."

The trip back to our place is quick, I'm pretty sure Core broke a few road rules to get us back here but I don't care. I need him and I need him now.

We race inside and head straight to our bedroom. I make quick work of my clothes; my body ablaze with want and need for him. Core stares at me and with his eyes locked on me, he pulls his shirt over his head in that sexy one-handed way that guys do. My gaze unashamedly roams his chest that was carved by the gods. He removes his jeans and briefs together. He's gloriously naked and my eyes once again roam over his body, I will never get enough of this man. His cock is hard and erect with the tip already glistening with precum. It makes my mouth water; I want to devour him. "Core, get your sexy as fuck ass over here now."

He growls at my swearing and that noise vibrates through my body. Who knew a sound like that could cause my body to react like this, but Corey-fucking-Cox does things to me. "I'd much rather watch your cock slide into my mouth but potato patatho."

He stares at me. The temperature in the bedroom rises the longer we eye fuck one another. "Get on your knees, Kitten."

"Why?" I ask, my heart rate increasing as he stalks naked toward me.

"Because I'm going to do exactly as you asked." He stops halfway to me. "I'm going to fuck your sassy mouth, and then I'm going to make love to my fiancé until the wee hours of the morning."

"You had me at fuck your mouth."

"Kitten," he growls.

With a wink, I drop to my knees and crawl toward him. Stopping at his feet, I gaze up at the man whom I love unconditionally. Licking my bottom lip, I bite it as I beckon him closer to me. His cock is right in front of me, the head weeping with his arousal. My tongue darts out and I swipe it across the tip. Core hisses and it turns into a groan when I suck his shaft into my mouth.

"Fuck, I love your mouth," he pants, as he guides my head back and forth. My eyes flick to the freestanding mirror and I watch our reflection as Core does exactly as he threatened: he fucks my mouth. And fuck me sideways, it's the hottest thing I've ever seen. I was wet before but watching ourselves in the mirror has me dripping with need. Sliding my hand down between my legs, I flick my piercing before slipping two fingers inside myself. I moan around his dick. I'm so turned on right now. I look back up at him and I look toward the mirror. He follows my gaze and I watch his cock slide in and out of my mouth. His gaze is a little lower and he watches my fingers glide in and out of my folds.

"You are fucking everything, Baylor Evans. You are mine. Now and forever," he groans, increasing his thrusts, causing me to choke on his dick. He pulls back and drops to his knees in front of me. He grips my cheeks. "You okay, Kitten?"

Nodding my head, I cover his hands with mine. "Better than ever. I fucking love you so much."

"Kitten," he growls, in that delicious way I've come to love.

"Fuck you," I sass at him. Falling to the carpet, I lie back and spread my legs open. My clit is swollen and throbbing, my fingers won't cut it anymore. "I need you, Core."

"You have me, Kitten," he says, as he slides his cock into me. My walls clench and hug him tight. "Fuuuuck," he groans. He drops forward and rests on his forearms. He fucks me like the stallion he is. He literally takes my breath away.

"Now!" he shouts and the two of us come together. Screaming each other's name as we tumble into that glorious orgasmic abyss.

Opening my eyes, I stare up at him. I love this man with all my heart and soul. Who knew getting arrested, going undercover, doing jail time, and a stint in WitSec would lead to all of this?

Falling for Agent Cox was the best decision I ever made.

Epilogue

WHEN BAYLOR SURPRISED me and proposed, she totally ruined what I had planned for the following week, so I had to quickly rearrange my plans but either way, we were engaged. And now, my Kitten and I are married and on our honeymoon. Avery and Flynn gifted us a trip to Oasis in Castaway Grove and it's fucking gorgeous, its literally an oasis. Not as gorgeous as my wife, but nothing is as gorgeous as her.

Lying in bed, I watch her sleep. My wife, I love saying that, is perfect in every way possible. She rolls over in her sleep, pulling the sheet down and baring her amazing tits to me. Sparkling in the morning sunlight is her engagement ring. The one I gave her after her surprise proposal, almost ruining mine...

...Leaving her sleeping, I quietly sneak out to the kitchen, I need to make a few adjustments and bring forward my proposal plans. I've just finished rearranging them and making coffee, when she slides her hands around my waist and kisses my shoulder blades. "Morning, fiancé."

"Morning, fiancée," I say back, spinning around to face her. I rest my hands on her lower back and stare into her gorgeous blue eyes. "Sleep well?"

"Like a baby. You?"

"Like a king."

"A king, hey, does that make me your queen?" As soon as she says this, her face drops. That was what Kye used to always say to her, not wanting her to be upset, I shake my head.

"You are my Kitten and my fiancée."

"Well, you are mine and my fiancé." She grins at me. "Is it just me, or is it fucking awesome to say fiancé?"

"Watch your mouth, Kitten."

"I know how you can shut me up."

"You are insatiable," I tell her, as I slide my hands down her purple satin nightie and cup her ass. "I always want you but I need you to get dressed. I have a surprise."

"I like surprises. What is it?"

"If I tell you, it won't be a surprise."

She pouts, "You can spank me."

"I can do that anytime I want, now if you behave, I will spank and cuff you later."

"Promises, promises," she says, as she pulls away from me, turns, and walks out of the kitchen. She stops at the entrance and clears her throat. Lifting my gaze, the minx is standing there naked, her nightie hanging from her index finger.

I'd love nothing more than to ravage her, but my surprise will be here in ten minutes and for what I have in mind, I need more than ten minutes.

"You are going to be the death of me, woman. Go and get dressed and I promise, later."

"You better, fiancé, otherwise I'm taking back my proposal."

"No take backsies!" I shout as she stomps, yes, stomps away.

Picking up my mug, I bring it to my lips and shake my head.

When she returns she's dressed in jeans that look like they were painted on and a purple halter top thingy. My eyes roam over her and when I get to her face, she's smirking. "Like what you see?"

Nodding, I hand her a coffee. "Fuck yes, I do."

"Watch you—" She doesn't get to finish because the doorbell rings. "You expecting someone?" she asks, as she walks to the door. She swings it open and the doorway is filled with a balloon bouquet of at least twenty balloons in different shades of purple. It's attached to a box, filled with grape taffy.

"Core," she coos, "you shouldn't have."

When she turns around, I'm down on bended knee with a ring box in my hand. "Baylor, you may have beaten me to the punch with the proposal, but mine has all the romance and taffy you could desire. I think I fell for you the moment I heard you sassing at Agent Hall, I've fallen more and more in love with you each and every day since then, and I will do so until my last breath. Baylor Martine Evans, Kitten, will you marry me?"

A tear cascades down her cheek and she drops to her knees in front of me. She grips my cheeks and slams her lips to mine. She kisses me deeply, knocking us back to the floor with her on top of me. "Is that a yes?" I ask against her lips.

"Yes, a thousand times, yes."

Rolling her to her back, I remove the ring from the box and slip it onto her finger. "I love you, Kitten."

"I love you too, Core."

…What are you grinning at?" she asks, bringing me back to the present.

"Remembering the day I asked you to marry me."

"That was the second best day of my life."

"The best being when you officially became Baylor Cox?"

"Nope," she says, shaking her head, "The best was the day I was arrested because it led me on the path to you."

"Who knew an arrest could lead to all this?" I ask her.

"Certainly not me. What shall we do today?"

"Weeeeelll," I draw the word out. "We are on our honeymoon and your ass is looking mighty fine. I was thinking a spanking."

"How about we work on my ass's tan and then tonight, you can turn it pink after I suck your cock."

"I fucking love your dirty mouth," I tell her, pulling her into me and kissing her deeply.

"And I fucking love you."

The spanking comes sooner than anticipated due to my wife's sassy mouth, and with her ass nice and pink, we change into our swimwear and head downstairs to work on her ass tan and have a few cocktails.

We are walking toward our cabana when an old friend and I run into each other. "Burton fucking Hayes, what are you doing here?" I say, as we do the one-armed bro backslap hug.

"I live here now, man. I bought Castaway Coffee."

"No shit."

"Yes, shit."

My eyes dart around, "Did Trina come too?"

He shakes his head. "Nah, we split. That's one of the reasons I came here."

"You finally woke up and saw the light, eh?" Trina was a crazy bitch, always out for herself. I always got the feeling she was hiding something but I never said anything 'cause Burton seemed happy.

"You could say that." His demeanor changes slightly but just as quickly, his face lights up when a gorgeous brunette walks toward us. "Hey, baby," she says, snuggling into his side. She looks to me and stretches out her hand, "Hey, I'm Nix"

"Corey," I say, placing my hand in hers and shaking. For a small thing, she has a good grip.

She turns her head to look up at Burton, love radiating between the two of them. "Kain is here, he and Talia just had another argument."

"Again?" Burton questions

"Yeah, those two just need to fuck already. Like seriously, penis in vagina, pump and repeat. Once they fuck away the tension, peace will return to the grove. Blind fucking Freddy can see they want each other, but they are too stubborn to see it."

"Love blinds some people, they don't see it until it smacks them up the side of the head when they least expect it."

"Are we speaking from experience?" Nix asks me.

Nodding, I grin. "Yeah. My Kitten came into my life when I least expected it."

"No shit," Burton says, "Agent Corey Cox has finally met 'the one.'"

"After he arrested me," my gorgeous wife says, sliding her arm around my waist joining us.

"You and I are going to get along smashingly," Nix says.

Burton rolls his eyes and whispers, "Ohh shit." He looks to Bay. "If she offers you a cocktail, run the other way."

"What can I say, I make killer cocktails." Nix nonchalantly shrugs but the look she is giving Burton right now is carnal and heated, it's similar to how Baylor looks at me when she wants to get down and dirty…or kill me.

There's a fine line between love and hate and Baylor and I walk along that precarious knife's edge each and every day. Baylor is my complete opposite but at the same time, she's my missing piece. Our love and hate collided spectacularly but I wouldn't change a thing. Well, maybe the getting shot part but the recovery blow jobs were amazing, so yeah, I'll keep the getting shot part.

"Killer, more like downright dangerous," Burton mumbles, but loud enough for all of us to hear.

"You love them…and me." Nix winks at him and then links arms with Bay, dragging her toward the Grove Bar. Like the lovesick puppies that Burton and I are, we follow them.

After way too many of Nix's killer cocktails, Baylor and I stumble toward the beach. We collapse into a cabana and snuggle into one another. We stare up at the night sky. There are a million tiny little stars twinkling in the night sky. "Core, you think that somewhere up there is a couple like us, snuggling and in love?"

"I've never really thought about it," I tell her, "But I do know that I'm happy to be snuggling here with you." Rolling to face her, I rest my head on my hand. Brushing a tendril of hair off her face, I lean in and kiss her nose. "I love you, Baylor Cox."

"I love hearing that," she tells me.

"I love you," I repeat.

She shakes her head, "No, not that. I love that I'm officially Baylor Cox. If you had told me the first day we met that I'd be married to you, I would have told you to drop the crack pipe. Never in my wildest dreams did I think this would happen but seriously, getting arrested was the best thing to ever happen to me, because it led me to you."

"Arresting you was the best arrest of my life."

"Technically Hall and Oats arrested me. You just needed me to bring down the bad guy."

"Potato patahto. But you know what?"

"What?"

"I wouldn't change a thing either. Falling for you was the best thing I ever did."

"Aww, you say such sweet things. Now, take me back to our room and fuck me."

"Watch your mouth, Kitten."

She leans over and kisses me, "You wouldn't have me any other way. Now, let's go."

It's true, I love her just the way she is.

THE END!!!!!

To see how Avery and Flynn got together, grab Falling for Dr. Kelly.

Every force has an equal and opposite attraction.
Love being the most volatile of them all.

AVERY
My life is anything but boring.
So what if I'm an introvert and prefer to focus on my career?
I was fine.
Until I met him—Flynn Kelly.
The doctor with the sexy Irish accent.
I thought we were unbreakable, until someone close hurts me in an unimaginable way.
Can two opposites fight the laws of attraction or will it end up tearing us apart?

FLYNN
I work hard, and play even harder.
When it came to women, I could have anyone I want.
Until I met her—Avery Evans.
She's quiet, shy, and everything I'm not.
But we're drawn together like magnets, sparking each other to life.

When the unthinkable happens, our differences really show. Is our attraction about to sizzle and flame out? Only time will tell.

To find out what happens with Lexi, Preston and Cress, grab Falling for Dr. Knight.

Falling
for
Dr. Knight

Chaos and tragedy can either bring us together, or tear us apart.
Falling in love isn't like it is in fairy tales.

CRESSIDA
Being a single mom is hard.
But Lexi is my life, and I'll do anything for my daughter.
I just never expected tragedy to strike, or for my past to haunt us.
Or for Dr. Preston Knight to be the man who saves us.
The same man I should *never* have fallen in love with.

PRESTON
I'm the best in my field.
Being a doctor is in my *blood*.
My focus is always on my career.
Until her—Cressida Bayliss.
I've fought many battles, but never one so close to my heart.
This is the biggest fight of my life, and with my heart on the line, I can't afford to lose.

Charli was betrayed by her partner. When she's assigned a new one, sparks fly...but can she trust him? Find out of she can in

Falling
for
Agent Cruz

There's no rhyme or reason when it comes to happily ever afters.
Falling in love happens when you least expect it.

CHARLI
I was betrayed, now I don't trust easily.
One night I let loose and do something crazy.
When my new partner is assigned, I'm shocked to find we've already met.
From the moment my eyes land on him, I know I'm screwed.
Dominic Cruz crashes through my fortress and I start to trust again.
Until I don't.
Then I discover something that will change everything.

DOMINIC
This new assignment fell into my lap.
I was reluctant but then I met my new partner—Charli Davis.
The one who rocked my world and left in the middle of the night.

Our connection was instant and it's still as intense.
My future is finally looking bright.
Then my past finds me.
Now everything is uncertain, but nothing is as it seems.

Acknowledgments

After eighteen books, writing these never get any easier. I'm always scared I will forget someone. It takes a team to write a book and I'm so lucky to have a fantabolous team behind me.

Tara Lee, thank you for talking me off the ledge. You words of encouragement meant the world to me. You are a fellow author but you are also my friend, why do you live so far away?

Andi, Andi, Andi…what would I do without you? You are my sounding board, advice giver and suggestion queen. Your messages as you read chapter by chapter always make me smile, especially when you yell at me. #SorryNotSorry

To my beta babes, **Andi, Bec, Jenny, Tara** and **Stefanie,** I love and appreciate you ladies so much. Your honesty helped make this book everything that it is AND Bec and Jenny, told you both that I'd redeem Baylor.

My editor, **Karen**, from **Barren Acres Editing;** I'm running out of things to say. You're not only my editor, but you're also a great friend; why do you live so far away? Thank you, once again for helping me turn my book baby from a pile of crap into a beautiful book baby.

My cover designer, **Ally**. Thank you for the beautiful covers, as soon as I saw them, I knew I wanted them for the Falling special editions.

Thank you to **Zai** from **Heart Full of Reads Editing Services** for checking my I's are dotted and my T's are crossed. No matter how many times I read it, I always miss a few.

To the following authors; **Rebecca Barber, Chloe Renee, Stefanie Jenkins, Renee Linda, Tara Lee, Linda Higgins, Alana Jade, Elle Thorpe** and **Cass Fowler;** thank you for your support, encouragement and writing sprints. Without you guys, I'd be a mess in the corner drinking wine from my coffee mug.

I know they'll never read this, but thank you **Stephen Amell** and **Vanessa Hessler** for being my muses for Corey and Baylor. I've never really had a clear picture of my characters before I start writing but this time, you guys were at the forefront of my mind while writing. Thank you for helping me bring Corey and Baylor to life.

And finally **you, my readers**; thank you for the kind words that you message me with each release. 9 out of 10 times, these arrive just when I need a pick me up and they always do. From the bottom of my heart, thank you for supporting me and my books.

Cheers,

Dana Xo

Also by DL Gallie

STAND ALONES

Antecedent

Doc Steel

Oops

Off the Books

Fractured: A driven world novel

Deck…the Balls

Secrets and Sunrises

Always in the Cards

Out of Nowhere

Love Me Like You Do

Never Let Me Go

Seven Nights

Seven Kisses

After the Ashes

PUCKING NOVELS

I Pucking Hate That I Love You

A Pucking Good Christmas

…and a few pucking more

FALLING NOVELS

These men make it hard not to fall for them

Falling for Dr. Kelly

Falling for Dr. Knight

Falling for Agent Cox

Falling for Agent Cruz

Falling:The Complete Collection

THE UNEXPECTED SERIES

When it comes to love, expect the unexpected

The Unexpected Gift

The Unexpected Letter

The Unexpected Package

The Unexpected Connection

The Unexpected series: The Complete Collection

THE CASTAWAY GROVE COLLECTION

Love has arrived in the Grove

Oasis

Unequivocal Love

Five Words

Broken Rules

…and a few more to come.

The Castaway Grove Collection, Vol 1

THE LIQUOR CABINET SERIES

Liquor has never been so disturbingly saucy

Malt Me (Book 1)

Tequila Healing (Book 2)

Wine Not (Book 3)

The Final Shot (Book 4)

The Liquor Cabinet: Series boxset

FACEBOOK ~ INSTAGRAM ~ BOOKBUB

GOODREADS ~ WEBSITE

dlgallieauthor@outlook.com

Sign up to my newsletter

About the Author

DL Gallie is from Queensland, Australia, but she's lived in many different places all over the world, including the UK and Canada. She currently resides in Central Queensland with her husband and two  munchkins. She and her husband have been together since she was sixteen, and although they drive each other crazy at times, she couldn't imagine her life without him.

Shortly after her son was born, DL began reading again. With encouragement from her husband, she picked up the pen and started writing, and now the voices in her head won't shut up.

DL enjoys listening to music, drinking white wine in the summer, red wine in the winter, and beer all year round. She's also never been known to turn down a cocktail, especially a margarita.